By ANDREW (

Accompanied by a Waltz
Between Loathing and Love
Can't Live Without You
Chasing the Dream
Crossing Divides
Dominant Chord
Dutch Treat
Eastern Cowboy
Eyes Only for Me
In Search of a Story
The Lone Rancher
North to the Future
One Good Deed
Path Not Taken
Planting His Dream
Rekindled Flame
Saving Faithless Creek
Shared Revelations
Stranded • Taken
Three Fates (Multiple Author
Anthology)
To Have, Hold, and Let Go
Turning the Page
Whipped Cream

HOLIDAY STORIES
Copping a Sweetest Day Feel
Cruise for Christmas
A Lion in Tails
Mariah the Christmas Moose
A Present in Swaddling Clothes
Simple Gifts
Snowbound in Nowhere
Stardust

ART
Legal Artistry • Artistic Appeal
Artistic Pursuits • Legal Tender

BOTTLED UP
The Best Revenge
Bottled Up • Uncorked
An Unexpected Vintage

BRONCO'S BOYS
Inside Out • Upside Down
Backward • Round and Round

THE BULLRIDERS
A Wild Ride • A Daring Ride
A Courageous Ride

BY FIRE
Redemption by Fire
Strengthened by Fire
Burnished by Fire
Heat Under Fire

CARLISLE COPS
Fire and Water • Fire and Ice
Fire and Rain • Fire and Snow

CHEMISTRY
Organic Chemistry
Biochemistry • Electrochemistry

Published by
DREAMSPINNER PRESS
www.dreamspinnerpress.com

By ANDREW GREY

Published by
DREAMSPINNER PRESS
www.dreamspinnerpress.com

CAN'T LIVE WITHOUT YOU

ANDREW GREY

Published by
DREAMSPINNER PRESS

5032 Capital Circle SW, Suite 2, PMB# 279, Tallahassee, FL 32305-7886 USA
www.dreamspinnerpress.com

Can't Live Without You
© 2016 Andrew Grey.

Cover Art
© 2016 L.C. Chase.
http://www.lcchase.com
Cover content is for illustrative purposes only and any person depicted on the cover is a model.

ISBN: 978-1-63477-756-8
Digital ISBN: 978-1-63477-757-5
Library of Congress Control Number: 2016909431
Published September 2016
v. 1.0

Printed in the United States of America

This paper meets the requirements of
ANSI/NISO Z39.48-1992 (Permanence of Paper).

To Dominic, because I can't live without you in my life.

CHAPTER 1

"AREN'T YOU ready yet?" Ethan asked in a slightly whiny voice that only he could make sound unchildish. Maybe it was the slight head tilt and the way he stuck his lip out just so that made the effect work every damn time. Guys in Hollywood seemed to know how to be annoying without being annoying. At least that was what Roy, Justin's agent, had said once.

"I don't think I want to go," Justin Hawthorne said as he stood in front of his huge closet without seeing anything inside.

"You have to go—the party is for you. It's to celebrate the fact that your latest movie went into the stratosphere and you're going to be the star of the next decade."

Ethan nudged him aside and started going through his clothes. He knew where everything was in Justin's closet because he was the one who organized it, just like he pretty much organized everything and everyone in Justin's life. Not that that was a bad thing. Justin was busy and never seemed to have time for the mundane things in life. Just once he'd like to be able to cook a meal, sit down, and eat it in peace. Instead he had people who did all the cooking for him. Hell, if his agent could figure out how to have people eat, piss, and take a crap for him, he'd outsource those functions as well.

"You pushed me into agreeing to go the party, and I'm tired as hell. I've been on three talk shows and two nighttime shows, and I'm supposed to start shooting another movie in a week. I don't want to go to some loud club with music that gives me a headache. I want to stay home for one night this week, put my feet up on the very expensive furniture that you picked out, close my eyes, and have ten minutes to breathe." He added a snap to the end of his sentence to accentuate his point.

Ethan stopped his rummaging and turned to face him. "Do you want something to relax you?"

Ethan left the closet at his usual frenetic pace, reached into his jacket pocket, and pulled out a small case. As he opened it and pulled out a pill, Justin, without thinking, swung his arm to bat it away. He caught the container, sending it flying and the contents scattering across the plush carpet.

"I don't want any pills, and if you're going to turn into a drug dealer, you can fucking leave and not come back!" Justin had seen what happened to people once Hollywood got its hands on them. Immensely talented people chewed up and spat out by chemicals and their consequences. He pointed toward the door. "You know I will not have that."

"It's over the counter. Geez. I know how you feel about that stuff." Ethan gathered up the pills and was about to drop them in the trash can, but instead he went into the bathroom and flushed them down the toilet.

"Thank you, and no, I don't want anything other than a rest." He needed to get it under control.

"You really are jumpy," Ethan said as he went back to the closet. "Go sit down for a few minutes. I'll find you something to wear, and you can come in to change in twenty minutes."

Justin twisted his finger in the air. A whole twenty minutes on his own, whatever would he fucking do with himself? He didn't argue, though, and left the bedroom, wandering to his glass-walled living room, which overlooked his incredibly manicured lawn and the lighted pool that shimmered and glistened in the night. He pulled open one of the glass doors, and the gentle hum of the waterfall that tumbled into the far side of the rock-lined pool drifted inside. He loved that sound. It was one of the few places in the entire city that reminded him of the hometown he'd left years before.

Sometimes he wondered what his life would have been like if he'd stayed in Biglerville, Pennsylvania, after graduation. He'd probably have ended up working in one of the fruit-processing plants, just like half the people he knew. Justin sat in one of the huge chairs, then stood up once again. The damn things looked wonderful but felt like shit when he sat in them. He moved to the sofa and propped his sock clad feet on the glass coffee table.

God, this felt so damn good, just a few minutes of quiet.

Everything about LA was loud and zipped by at lightning speed. No one walked at a normal pace; they ran. At least it seemed that way most of the time. He always had to be one place and then another ten minutes later, hustled from limousine to studio and then back to the car to go someplace else. Still, the house was quiet, and he decided to take it in while he could.

"I found something wonderful for you to wear. I set it out on the bed for you."

Justin had closed his eyes, and he didn't open them. "Thank you." He could feel Ethan standing in the room and knew he wasn't moving. "I know what you're thinking, but it's my house and my coffee table, and if I want to put my feet on it, I will."

"But that's a—" Ethan began, probably about to name some furniture designer who was all the rage at the moment.

"It's a coffee table," Justin countered. "And it's mine. At least I paid for it." His house had been furnished like a film set and had been photographed and published in *People* magazine with him appearing happy and perfect. He lifted his feet and set them down again for emphasis. "I want ten minutes of quiet. That's all I ask."

"Okay," Ethan said, and Justin heard him sit in one of the other chairs. He kept his eyes closed, doing his best to ignore his best friend for just a little while. Ethan stood up again within seconds and left the room. He could never stay still for more than ten seconds and always had to be doing something. "Here," Ethan said when he returned. Justin cracked his eyes open and took the glass of grape juice that Ethan handed him. He drank, letting the sweetness slide down his throat.

"I'm tired, Ethan," Justin said, cradling the cold glass in his hands. "I've been going at a death-march pace for so long I don't have much energy left. I've done movie after movie, talk shows, television guest appearances, interviews. I've had people following me everywhere I go, and in fact, right now, there are people waiting out by the gate for me to go out tonight so they can try to take my picture. God knows why. Half the time I think they're trying to snap the photo of me picking my nose or burping because that's the most meaningful and human thing I do. Everything else is staged, scripted, primped, and pouffed."

"Do you really not want to go tonight?" Ethan asked. "I'll call and…."

"No. I'll go because I said I would." He always did his best to meet commitments. That was one of the things his grandfather had drilled into him. *Son, always do what you say you're going to do. That's part of what makes you a man.* "But I need you to find me a way to get out of there after no more than two hours. I'm not going to sit there all night. That's your one job tonight. Two hours and then I'm going home."

"But—" Justin glared at him, and Ethan nodded. "Got it. Two hours."

Justin raised himself off the sofa and went to his bedroom, then closed the door. He found the clothes and stripped down. He checked his face in the mirror and shaved for the second time that day. He rarely looked scruffy because of his naturally blond hair, but every flaw showed in pictures, so he did it. Everything had to be clean and perfect.

Once he was cleaned up and dressed, he checked himself one more time and then stepped out of the room. Ethan was waiting by the door and fussed with his collar. "You look wonderful."

Justin hugged his friend because he thought they both needed it, then stepped back. He blinked a few times. "Is that what you're wearing?"

"Yes. No one is going to be looking at me." Ethan was dressed in nice gray slacks and a light blue shirt. It was nice enough, but plain.

"Is that how you always dress?" Justin asked, realizing for the first time that he rarely noticed how his best friend dressed.

"Sure," Ethan answered. "I'm like the wallpaper."

"Not tonight," Justin said and went back into his bedroom. He pulled open one of the lower dresser drawers and came up with what he was looking for. "Put this on. It was a gift from some awards show last year, and the sleeves were too short." It was a deep red silk shirt from some designer Justin could never remember. "Try it on." He handed it to Ethan, who smiled widely as he took the shirt.

The fabric shimmered in the light, and Justin leaned back as his friend unbuttoned his shirt and slipped on the new one. "How does it feel?"

"Luxurious," Ethan said.

"Good. Then take it. It was made for someone with your coloring." Ethan had the coloring that came from his Italian background, with raven black hair and an olive tone to his skin. "I used to wonder why you and I never got together," Justin said as Ethan finished dressing.

"Because we're best friends and that's how we work best. Besides, I think we both like to be in charge in the bedroom."

Ethan raised his eyebrows, and Justin laughed as he wondered why he didn't remember that. He tried to remember Ethan's birthday. It was sometime in August, but the date escaped him. He'd been so busy that he was missing important things about the people in his life.

"What?" Ethan asked.

Justin realized he'd been staring. "I've been so busy I haven't even been seeing you." He took a single step closer. "I doubt I've been seeing anything or anyone around me. All I do is go from place to place or set to set, and I'm tired all the damn time."

"I get that. But you know this is a fickle town—you can be on top one minute and in the dump the next. So you have to make the most of the good times."

"Yes. But what if you're running so fast that the good times are a blur?"

Ethan nodded. "Maybe you need a vacation. As you said, you're not shooting for a week. Take some time off and go somewhere fun. I can put together some ideas, and you could leave tomorrow."

God, that was enticing. "I'd like to…." Justin checked his watch. "If we're going to go, we should probably leave now or we'll be late." Justin waited for Ethan to leave the room and turned out the lights before following him to the garage. He had three cars: a BMW, a Ford Edge for when he didn't want to be noticed, and a Ferrari. He headed right for the bright yellow Italian sports car and slid easily into the driver's seat. Ethan got in the passenger seat, and once the doors were closed, Justin raised the garage door and pulled out.

"Are you going to put the top down?"

"No, I don't want any pictures tonight." He pulled out and lowered the door behind him, then started down the drive, pushing the button to open the gate.

There were indeed photographers, and one of them stood right in the middle of the drive. "That son of a bitch," Ethan exclaimed.

Justin pulled to a stop, gunned the engine, and then released the clutch just enough that the car jerked forward a foot or so. The photographer dove for the bushes, and Justin sped off while Ethan pressed the button to close the gate. "Call the security service and have them sweep by to make sure one of those morons doesn't try to scale the gate or something," Justin told him.

"Already on it," Ethan said as Justin gunned the engine, the hum and power thrumming through him. He listened to Ethan make his call as he made his way out of the hills and down to Sunset Boulevard. "I love this car."

"Me too." Justin drove as fast as he dared. Traffic built as he got closer to the club. He glided to a stop right in front and got out. The valet came around and took the car for him. Justin waved to people on the sidewalk as he walked toward the entrance. A lot of people he knew would have hurried inside the safety of the club, but Justin didn't on principle. The camera flashes were almost blinding, but he walked at a normal pace. He stopped when he saw a young woman of about eighteen and then walked over to her.

"Hello," he said when he got close enough that she could hear him. "What's your name?"

She grinned and bounced up and down. "Ally."

"Are you having a fun night?"

"I am now," she said.

Ethan was right behind him and handed him an index-sized card and a pen. Justin wrote a note to Ally, signed the card, and leaned over to give her a kiss on the cheek. "I'm glad." He handed her the card and continued on into the club as everyone else screamed for his attention.

The thump of the music surrounded him as he stepped inside. "Mr. Hawthorne," one of the bouncers said. He was huge but wore a smile. "Your party is right this way. If you'll follow me."

"Thank you." He followed the large man with Ethan behind him, threading between tables and the milling crowd. It was dark, and there were enough other distractions that he wasn't recognized.

"Justin," a familiar voice said as a hand gently touched his arm. "How have you been?"

He turned and was engulfed in a hug. "Kevin. I'm fine. How are you?" He hugged Kevin back briefly and stepped away. His ex—distant ex, thank God—had no respect for personal boundaries.

"Really good. Things are taking off for me, and I'm doing really well." Of course he was. Kevin was now one of the "it" party people. If there was a party, he was there. If a party needed to be started, just call Kevin. He could arrange for it all… and Justin knew that meant just about anything. "We should get together for old time's sake. Have some fun." He got too close once again.

"Maybe sometime," Justin said, being noncommittal and trying to figure the quickest way out of this without causing a scene.

"Don't worry. I'll bring everything and everyone." He waggled his eyebrows, and Justin stifled a groan. "We used to have so much fun. Remember?"

Justin did remember, and he'd put a stop to that pretty quickly, stepping away from that scene and putting distance between him and Kevin when he found out exactly what was going on at Kevin's parties. "I have to meet some friends for the evening. I'll see you later." Thankfully a woman was trying to get Kevin's attention, and he used those few seconds to escape.

He and Ethan passed through the rest of the main portion of the club to a private room where a number of friends and acquaintances were waiting, including his agent, Roy Fisher, and a number of people Justin had worked with.

"I was starting to think you weren't going to show up," Roy said as he took his arm and tried to steer him away from the crowd. Justin was ready for the move and whirled away from him.

"Unless it's urgent, as in life and your impending death, I don't want to discuss business tonight." Roy tended to use social situations as business meetings. "Call me tomorrow and we'll talk over what you have."

"Have a drink," Ethan said and stuck a glass into Roy's hand.

"I have a huge deal for when you finish your next picture," Roy said, leaning close. "The payday is twenty million." Roy looked like he was going to do some kind of happy dance.

"That will send your kids to college," Justin said without humor. Roy was a good agent, but he was also all about the money. That came first, and Justin knew it. That was also why he had an independent accountant with a large firm who followed up on every dime. He was not going to show up on the news as one of those pathetic Hollywood stories—the person who'd made millions, done all the work, and ended up broke because he'd trusted the wrong people. Justin did trust the people he worked with, but he also verified that he was being told the truth. "Come to the house at eight tomorrow and we'll discuss it… unless you want to join me for my workout."

Roy paled. "Fine, eight it is. I'll bring breakfast."

Justin patted him on the shoulder and moved into the party, greeting friends and shaking hands.

"I'll get you another drink," Ethan said. He was the only person Justin trusted enough to get him anything that he didn't see go into the glass. His life was one huge caution flag.

"Thanks," Justin said, and Ethan threaded off through the crowd.

"Sweetheart," Lila Montagne said as she hurried up to him, wrapping an arm around his waist. She smelled of alcohol, and Justin could tell she had already had too many. When she leaned into him, he had to help her stand. "We worked so well together." She hiccupped and tilted his way. Thankfully she weighed next to nothing. "I hope we can do it again in the future."

"Me too, sweetheart."

She hiccupped once more and was hit with a fit of the giggles. "It's too bad you're gay or I'd be all over you." She stood up straight, eyes glassy but her gaze relatively steady. "Wanna give the other side a try?"

She made a grab for him, and Justin stepped back. He wasn't about to get his balls grabbed by a drunken starlet. He wanted them in one piece, and Lila was known for going after what she wanted whole hog, as it were.

"No, thanks, but you're a good friend." He kissed her cheek the same way he had the girl out front. Ethan returned and handed him a drink, and then Justin escorted Lila to a chair, where she collapsed in a heap. "This is what you wanted me to come for?" he asked Ethan.

"No. It was for him," Ethan said and pointed to Justin's supporting actor in *Runaway*. He stood off to the side with a few people talking to him, but otherwise everyone was doing their thing.

"Alexander," Justin called as he approached him. Alexander smiled, and they hugged in a real manly way. Alexander was as straight as they came, and he'd been standoffish when they started the film, but by the end they were friends. "Thanks for doing this. It's a great party."

"Thanks," Alexander said. He turned toward a woman with a clipboard standing off to the side of the bar. "It was my publicist's idea, but I'm glad you came. It was great working with you."

Working together, he and Alexander had found they had more in common than either of them expected. Alexander had come from a small town and seemed on his way up.

"I took your advice. My agent had a fit, but he knows not to mess with me."

"And you can sleep at night," Justin said.

"Yeah," Alexander agreed.

Justin sipped from his martini glass and was pleased to taste only cold water. "What have you got next?"

"There's some talk about a lead in a couple features, but nothing else at the moment. You know how things are. It will take a little time and then hopefully things will bust open. You?"

"The next big deal. I start shooting on a sort-of *Beowulf* adventure. Costumes, women in saucy clothes, the works. It's a great story, and it should be fun. We're talking about the project after that. I'll work with you anytime, and I passed on the word to some directors I know. You're professional, on time, and good at what you do. You'll be getting some calls."

"Thanks, Justin," Alexander said.

Other people called out, and Justin shook hands with the guys in Alexander's crowd, then continued working the room. He talked to everyone, saying hello and shaking hands. He never knew when a good impression was going to be required, and he was damned sure to make one.

"Do you ever relax?" Ethan asked once Justin was able to stop talking and had finished his glass of water.

He leaned close to Ethan. "No. You have to remember that for the most part, these people aren't my friends. They're partygoers, hangers-on, and people trying to get a leg up in the business. They all want something from me."

"That's pretty cynical."

"Reality. I want something from them too, and I'm going to get it. Each of these people will see me and talk to me. I'll be nice, pleasant, and they'll have a positive opinion of me. Then I can go home and they can get drunk off their asses, fuck a stranger, and have their pictures in the tabloids while I'm in bed, getting rested for work."

Ethan shook his head, but Justin definitely saw more than a little admiration. "You always wanted it bad and were willing to do what it took." Ethan weaved his way back to the bar, and Justin headed toward the one corner of the room he hadn't visited yet.

"John," Justin said and shook hands with the director of *Runaway*. "Glad to see you here." Ethan pressed a glass into his hand and joined the group. "This is my best friend and mother hen. Ethan, this is John Westhoffer."

"You did an amazing job on *Runaway*. Some of the shots and the setups were unbelievable. Your vision for the film was stunning and so far reaching."

"Thank you," John said with a grin. "I love to plan out my films in a lot of detail, but I also think it's important to give good actors their head and let them add themselves to the part. Justin here is a natural at making a character come to life."

"Ethan would love to work behind the camera," Justin said, and Ethan nudged him in the arm. "He has a great eye and thinks much the same way you do." He smiled. "Remember that first day, when we were on two different planets?"

"God, yes. I thought I was going to have an ulcer if the entire film was that difficult, and then the next day you came in and it was like we were in perfect sync and you got the vision."

"Ethan got your vision when I told him what was happening. He helped get my head in the right space."

John nodded and then reached into his pocket and handed Ethan a card. "Call me this week and set up an appointment. We need to talk." John excused himself.

Ethan nearly fell over. "No way," he said, practically jumping up and down.

"Yes." Justin smiled and sipped his water. He felt his phone vibrate in his pocket. He pulled it out, checked the number, and handed it to Ethan, who answered it. Ethan continued talking, then tapped Justin on the shoulder and tilted his head toward the corner of the room. They stepped over, and Ethan handed the phone back.

"You need to take this call."

Ethan stepped away, and Justin lifted the device to his ear. "Yes?"

"Mr. Grove?" a strange man said, using Justin's real last name.

"How did you get this number?" He kept things like his cell phone number very private and personal.

"From your father. Mr. Grove, I'm Dr. Heath from Adams County Medical Center in Gettysburg, and I regret to inform you that your father is in critical care."

"I'm sorry to hear that, but I haven't spoken a word to my father in seven years. Did he tell you he disowned me? The bastard said he didn't have a son, and now, when he wants something…."

"Your father could die," Dr. Heath said, and Justin bit back the retort that threatened. "He asked me to call you."

"Why didn't he call himself?"

"Your father can't speak. He communicates through hand gestures and a few words. He wrote down this number, and it took him three tries to get all the numbers. He's very weak, and I honestly don't think he will last more than a few days. This call could be his dying wish." That was worthy of any screenwriter. "I told him I would try on his behalf."

Justin felt the pain of rejection and heard the vitriol and condescension from his father just like it was yesterday. "I'll have to think about it," he said. He was seconds from ending the call.

"Please do. I know you don't know me from Adam, but don't do something you might regret. Once your dad is gone, it will be too late for a second chance."

His father didn't deserve any kind of second chance as far as Justin was concerned. "I'll think about it. Thank you for calling." He hung up, jammed his phone in his pocket, and headed toward the bar. When he arrived, he set his glass aside and ordered a shot of tequila. "Keep them coming," he told the bartender.

"Are you sure about that?" Ethan asked from right behind him. "You have to drive home." Justin took the shot, downed it, and waved off another. He pulled a bill out of his pocket and placed it on the bar before turning to Ethan.

"Let's get out of here," Justin said and turned away from the bar. He did his best to do the meet-and-greet thing as he made his way to the door, but he needed to get out of there. The paparazzi were still outside, so Justin plastered on a smile as he called for his car. When it arrived, he got in, and as soon as Ethan closed his door, he pulled into traffic.

"What happened? Is there something wrong? The guy said he was a doctor and—"

"I'm fine. It's my father. He's dying." Justin sped up and drove into the hills toward home. He had to get away from everyone.

"The one who kicked you out?" Ethan asked as Justin pulled into the driveway. They had shared their stories when they first met, after Justin had arrived in LA with huge dreams and empty pockets. Ethan had taken him in, giving him a place to live while he waited tables at night and went to auditions during the day.

Justin got out of the car and went inside with Ethan following. "Yeah. The bastard who told me he was no longer my father has a doctor calling to say that the fucker is dying and I should go back to say good-bye or some shit." Justin went to his bedroom. He pulled off his clothes, leaving them on the bed, and yanked on a navy blue Speedo before running out through the sliding glass doors and diving into the water. He needed to cool off and leave it all behind. When he surfaced, he started swimming laps, and he felt when Ethan entered the pool. He drove all the hurt and pain from his mind as he pushed his body through the water. He had to clear away the old, get rid of it, so he could decide what he wanted to do.

Time had little meaning. He kept swimming until his arms and legs refused to move any longer. Then he glided to the side of the pool, where Ethan lay on one of the lounges, wrapped in a supersized bath sheet like a blanket against the cooler night air.

"What do you want to do?" Ethan asked without lifting his head off the back of the lounge.

"I haven't a fucking clue," Justin said, folding his arms over the edge of the pool and resting his chin on his hands. "My father disowned me, and my mother did nothing to stop him. He said I was no longer his son and that I wasn't welcome in his life. When my mother died, he never called me. He had my number from my mother because he used it today. The bastard cut me out completely, and now he wants something."

"Do you want to find out what it is?" Ethan asked. "If you do, we get on a plane and find out. It's as simple as that. Are you going to wonder, or can you simply let this all go?"

Justin settled back in the water, sinking to the bottom of the pool, letting the warmth surround him. Sometimes he needed a chance for the answers to come to him. When he was about to run out of air, he surfaced, swam to the steps, and climbed out. "I have a meeting with Roy at eight tomorrow morning. Book us on a flight to Baltimore that we can catch after the meeting. Reserve a car there, and we'll drive up." With that decision made, he got back into the pool and floated quietly, looking up at the few stars that permeated the LA light and haze.

Ethan's lounge scraped the concrete as he got up and then went inside the house. Justin floated for a while before getting out once again and wrapping himself in a towel. He padded inside and found Ethan on his laptop.

"There's a one o'clock with seats available. We'll get in late. Do you want to get the car and drive or spend the night first?"

"Get the car. It will be late there, but for us, it will be normal hours. Get a place to stay in Gettysburg. The hospital is there." Justin left Ethan to make the arrangements and went to his room to get ready for bed.

Living in the same house as Justin did have its advantages, like a very quick commute to and from work.

THE FLIGHT was indeed long. Justin used the time to read through the paperwork his agent had given him. There was a ton of legalese, but he wanted to look it over anyway. By the time the wheels touched down, Justin had napped, which was easy in his first-class seat, knowing that Ethan was there to stand guard.

In the airport, he let Ethan get the car. He'd pay for it on the credit card Ethan had on one of Justin's accounts. They loaded the luggage and Ethan drove out of the city, west to Frederick, then north to their hotel in Gettysburg. It was well after midnight by the time Ethan checked them in and they went to the large hotel room. Justin collapsed on the sofa of their suite. "I never thought I would be back here."

"Are you hungry?" Ethan asked as he picked up the phone, laying out the room service menu. "They close in ten minutes."

"Sure. Just order something for me." He lay back on the sofa and closed his eyes. This entire trip had been unsettling, and more than once he had second-guessed his decision. If he had stayed away, everything would have unfolded on its own, and he could have gone on with his life, never giving his father a second thought. Instead he'd let curiosity and some long-dormant sense of a family bond pull him into this jittery emotional quagmire.

"Great, thank you," Ethan said into the phone. Turning to Justin, he told him, "Food will be here in a little while. I'm going to get ready for bed, and we can eat when it gets here." He went into the bathroom after a flurry of going through his luggage. Justin stayed still until Ethan bounded out of the bathroom in shorts and a T-shirt.

Ethan was good-looking, lithe, energetic—a great catch. Justin wondered for the millionth time why nothing had happened between them. Even now as he watched him, Justin was surprised at his lack of desire. Ethan was like a brother to him and too important in his life to ever mess up with sex.

Justin rolled off the sofa and changed as well. By the time he was done, the tray of food had been delivered and was resting on the sitting area coffee table. Justin joined Ethan, and they ate quietly. Then Justin went into the bedroom.

He fell asleep almost instantly, waking because of a storm in the night that shook the building and pounded the windows with rain. Justin watched as lightning lit the room. His thoughts centered on his father and what he was going to find in the morning. Maybe his dad was already dead and this entire trip was a waste of time. It likely was anyway. It wasn't like his father had called himself to talk to him. He'd gotten someone else to do it. Who knew why? Maybe the doctor hadn't been telling the whole truth. Justin had no idea what was really going on. But the call out of the blue had unsettled him, and he hated it. He had a good life, one of his own making, and he was at the top of his profession. He didn't intend to let anything interfere with that life, especially not a father who had disowned him and now possibly felt guilty.

The storm inside his head abated just as the one outside the windows started moving on, and Justin rolled over, trying to go back to sleep in case another storm approached. One did as more and more rain moved through, but thankfully Justin barely heard it.

He woke to quiet and sunlight, warm and bright, streaming around the curtains. He slid out of the bed and put on his bathing suit and robe, then headed to the indoor pool.

The air, crisp and cool on his skin from the quick trip to the pool pavilion, didn't prepare him for the bracing chill of the water. His pool at home was heated to his exact specification. This one was heated, if to a colder temperature, but he slid into the water and began doing laps, letting his mind settle as he exercised.

"Justin," Ethan said after tapping him as he passed. "We need to get you inside and go."

"Why?"

"I was in the lobby, and people are already talking about how Justin Hawthorne is staying in the hotel. It's only going to take a few seconds before someone figures out it's you in the pool, and then you're going to be mobbed."

"Damn it." Justin climbed out of the water, pulled on his robe, and grabbed the towel to dry his hair. He walked toward the hotel, still drying his hair, right past a small group of girls milling through the lobby, giggling excitedly. He knew that sound and quickly pressed the button for the elevator. The doors opened and he stepped inside. They'd made it.

"I hate sneaking around," Justin said.

"You can always change before you meet them." Ethan smiled. "I didn't think you wanted to do it in your bathing suit, although those girls would think they'd died and gone to heaven." Ethan laughed. "And that thing you're wearing is pretty small and leaves very little to the imagination."

Justin rolled his eyes. "Yes, Mother," he quipped.

"You don't want to give those girls the wrong idea." Ethan burst into laughter as the elevator doors opened and they hurried down to their room.

Justin got changed while Ethan ordered breakfast, and after they ate, he and Ethan rode down to the lobby and he greeted the group of girls with smiles. They all squealed, and he signed something for each of them before leaving the hotel.

The trip to the hospital didn't take long. "Jaime Grove's room," Justin told the lady at the visitors' desk. She gave him the room number and looked at him twice before giving him directions. Justin wound his way through the corridors of the small hospital until he stood outside his father's room.

He hesitated in the hallway. He hadn't seen his father for seven years. Their last words had been beyond harsh and had ended in Justin crossing the entire country. They had meant the end of their family.

"You need to go inside," Ethan whispered. "I'll be out here, and if he gives you any trouble, just say the word and I'll smother him with a pillow." Ethan smiled.

Justin turned and stood in the doorway. His father lay on the bed, surrounded by machines and monitors. He wondered how they found room for anything else. He stepped inside and slowly approached the bed. His father looked much the same, only with more gray hair, and he hadn't shaved in a few days. There were lines and creases that hadn't been there when Justin left, and his father seemed much slighter. He must have lost considerable weight.

Justin opened his mouth to say something, anything, but his voice failed him. What the fuck should he say? He wanted to scream at him or tell him everything he'd done and throw his success in his father's face. Mostly he wanted to turn around and leave. He'd come this far and seen the old goat. Yes, he'd made the trip to see him before he kicked the bucket. He turned away and went back into the hall. "Let's go home," Justin said.

Ethan's eyes widened to dinner plates. "That's it? We came all this way for that?"

"I have nothing to say to him. I saw him, and that's enough."

"Is it really? Or are you afraid he's going to reject you all over again?" Ethan whispered harshly. "He can't do anything to you that you don't allow. He has no power over you, not anymore. You aren't a kid. You're a very successful adult who makes his own decisions and doesn't need his father any longer. Your father made sure of that when he kicked you out. So go on in there. Yell at him if you want. Tell him what a rotten father he was and that you deserved better. Say whatever it is that's been bottled up inside you for the last seven years and then tell him good-bye."

"I don't know if I can." Just being in the same room with him brought back all those memories. But Justin turned and went into the room, approaching his father's bed again. He stood there for a few minutes just looking at him. His father had always been so strong and forceful. Now he was weak and pale, the energy and force gone out of him, a shell of the person Justin remembered. "Father," Justin said formally. He'd stopped being his dad years earlier. His eyes remained closed, and Justin stood looking at the quiet figure.

Heavy footsteps sounded from behind him. Justin turned. "Georgie?" Justin said half under his breath, unable to believe what he was seeing. "Is that you?" His heart leaped for a second but then settled as the new reality overshadowed the old memories that seeing George had brought rushing back.

"Justin," George said in disbelief. "He told me he'd asked the doctor to call you." He came closer to the bed. "That was the last he spoke yesterday. Since then he's been still, and he hasn't opened his eyes."

"What happened?" Justin asked.

"He had a stroke a year ago and then a heart attack last week. Since then there's been a series of small incidents. They aren't calling them strokes, but that's what they act like. It's been up and down." George stood next to him. "They said there's only a slight chance he'll regain consciousness now."

So he hadn't made it in time. Not that Justin had been expecting anything. "Why are you here with him?"

"I've been taking care of your dad. I'm a home health care nurse, and after his heart attack he needed care, so I was called in."

"I bet that was uncomfortable," Justin said.

"Yes, it was at first. He didn't want to let me in the house, so I told him that was fine. He could sit in his chair and starve to death while he wet himself or he could let me in to help him. The old coot unlocked the door but refused to talk to me for a week."

"That sounds like him. Ignore what you don't like and maybe it will go away, no matter how good for you it may be." Justin kept his gaze on his father, hoping he'd open those damned eyes of his and say something to correct them, but of course he remained still.

"He's a stubborn ass if I ever saw one. But I took care of him, and eventually he opened up a little. Believe it or not, we became friends of a sort." George walked to the far side of the bed and checked the pillows as well as the monitors. "He's stable at the moment, but that's all anyone can say right now."

Justin nodded. "Has he ever said anything about…?" God, this was so fucking hard. He wanted to shake his father and ask him what in the hell possessed him to turn his back on his only child. Justin had only been honest with his father, something he had always told him was one of the most important things a man could be, and then he'd rejected Justin for doing exactly that.

"No. We talked about many things, but that day you left wasn't one of them," George said.

"He threw me out of the house," Justin said. "I told him who I was, and he turned his back on me." He stepped away from the bed and put his hands on his hips. "What I don't understand is how you can defend him in any way. After what happened… what he did… to me… to us."

"Yes, I know what he did. He kicked you out because he couldn't understand how his only son could be gay. But he didn't do anything to us. I was willing to stand by you through anything. You're the one who left, remember? You said good-bye and were out of town like a shot."

Justin lifted his gaze, looking across the bed to George. "There was…." He'd been so young, and people in town had sided with his father and turned their backs on him as well. "I didn't have a future here, remember? I asked you to come with me."

George nodded slowly. "You did. But I couldn't."

"You still had a family and people who loved you here. I didn't have that any longer."

"You had me," George said. "That should have been enough. But it wasn't. I know now that something else was calling you away. You had things you had to do, and I wasn't enough to keep you here. I understand that." George took a deep breath and grew quiet.

Justin took a few seconds to study the man who had been his first love. His eyes were the same—big, thoughtful, caring, and stunning, with green flecks in a clear blue-sky background. The rest of his face was older but still much the same, his features seemingly carved out of marble. The George he remembered had been lithe and fast, but he'd filled out and was wider and stronger now. A man, where in his memories George had always remained on the cusp of adulthood, with a hint of the boy that was gone now.

"We were so young," Justin said. "I don't know if I realized that then or not. We had our whole lives ahead of us, and so many dreams...."

"Justin?" his father whispered. His eyes were still closed, but his lips moved slowly. "Is that you?"

"Yes," he answered, pushing back the memories of confusion that talking about that time in his life always brought up. "I got a call from your doctor."

"You came." His eyes fluttered open. Justin looked into his father's eyes. They were cloudy, and he didn't know if his father really saw him or not. "I'm glad you did." He lifted his hand, and when Justin came closer, his father trailed his fingers down his arm until he found Justin's hand, then curled his fingers lightly around Justin's. "Thank you."

"For what?"

"I'm going to die."

"They told me," Justin said.

"At the end...." Justin had to strain to hear him. His father paused and his eyes closed. "We see the mistakes we made...." He took another breath, and his features tensed in pain and then relaxed. "In life. And we sometimes get a second chance." He released Justin's fingers. "You came," he repeated twice more, and then his features went slack, the pain leaving him completely along with his last breath of life. The last touch of his fingers fell away. A nurse came in and silenced the machines around him, leaving the room quiet.

Justin took a final look at his father, trying to reconcile his last words with his actions years before and coming up empty. He wanted to think that his father had known remorse for what he'd done. But he refused to believe that some sort of deathbed "I'm sorry" could make up for his father's rejection at a time when Justin had needed him most. He backed away from the bed and turned to leave the room.

"Will you be staying in town for very long?" George asked.

"I don't know. Do you know if he made any arrangements?" Justin didn't dare look at his father, so he watched George. Making funeral arrangements for a father who had disowned him wasn't a task he was looking forward to.

"Yes. Everything is done. All I have to do is call the funeral home, and they will know what to do." George came around the bed to where Justin stood. "He wanted to have everything planned and done. The only unfinished business he kept talking about was you."

"Then why didn't he call? He could have reached out a long time ago," Justin said. His father was dead. Anything said or unsaid was in the past now, he knew that. But he still had questions in light of what George was telling him.

"Would you have accepted his call?" George asked seriously.

"I don't know. He had the number. He could have used it. But he didn't until he knew he was dying, and then he was looking for some sort of forgiveness. I don't know if I can give that to him." The pain of having his family ripped away was too damn much even now.

"But in the end you came, and that's what he wanted most of all."

Justin peered deeply into the eyes he used to know so well. "What I really don't understand is how you could be his champion. He hurt both of us. Me most of all, but he didn't do you any favors either."

"Your father isn't the same person he was those years ago. The decisions he made weighed on him, and I came to understand the price he paid. Your dad was a lonely man the last years of his life, and he had no one to blame for that but himself. He came to understand and regret that." George sighed. "Anyway, we need to let the hospital take care of things."

He moved away from the bed and out of the room. Justin followed, and Ethan fell into step next to him.

"George, this is my friend Ethan Houghton. Ethan and I met when I landed in Los Angeles." He turned to Ethan. "Ethan, meet George Miller. George was my first love," he explained gently.

"How long were you planning to stay?" George asked after shaking hands with Ethan.

"I hadn't really thought that far ahead. Probably a few days," Justin answered. "I thought we could see where I grew up, and I'll stay through the funeral and then go back."

George nodded. "Things at home are pretty much the same as always. I have some things I need to take care of here, but I can meet you at the Lincoln Diner at noon, if you like."

"Thanks," Justin said. "We'll see you there."

Justin turned and headed down the corridor. His father had died, and yet he had no part in it. All the arrangements had been made, and all he needed to do was go to the funeral so he could lay things to rest between them. Things with his father had always hung over him, as much as he wanted to say they didn't.

"Are you going to be okay?" Ethan asked him as they approached the elevator.

Justin turned and saw George standing near the doorway to the room where his father lay, watching him. He was so tall and strong. As much as Justin could try to deny it, George had entered his soul when he was eighteen, and he'd never left. There had been very few days when Justin hadn't thought about the man now standing a few yards away, watching him intently as Justin stared back. While they waited for the elevator, Ethan was watching George too.

"Yes," Justin answered firmly, with more bravado than he felt. "Why wouldn't I be?" The door opened, and he stepped inside. "I hadn't seen or spoken to my father in many years. He disowned me, and now he's dead." He shrugged.

"I know when you're playing a part," Ethan said as the doors slid closed behind them, and Justin wondered just how much Ethan could read him.

CHAPTER 2

GEORGE MILLER entered the Lincoln Diner early and found a table in the back. He sat down, and one of the servers approached, wearing the little white lace hair covering popular with Mennonite women. They went about their business but were rarely overly friendly—polite to a fault, but not effusive the way many diner servers were.

"I'd like some coffee, please, and two other people will be joining me," he told her, and she hurried away, then returned to set up two other places.

George was both nervous and excited to see his old friend again. The truth was, he'd followed Justin's career ever since it had started. The guest appearances on television episodes were all recorded, and of course he'd seen all Justin's movies, including the one where he'd appeared nude in a love scene. That one he'd played many times, remembering when he'd seen Justin in real life, strong as day and as radiant as the sun. How many times had he imagined Justin returning home? He'd lost count over the years. Even though he knew he had no right to hope, and even if Justin were to return, it wasn't like he'd remember him.

Los Angeles was full of stunning men, and Justin was famous and out of the closet. That hadn't dimmed his popularity for a second. But George was no fool. Justin would have men throwing themselves at him all the time. He was a star, and George was just someone from his past. Nothing more.

He saw Justin's friend first. Ethan approached the table and then let Justin sit before sliding in next to him.

"I remember this place," Justin said. "We used to come here most Friday nights. Are the milkshakes still the same?"

The light in Justin's eyes captivated George, exactly the way it had before.

"They make them the same way," George said.

Justin slapped his hand on the table and smiled huge and happy as he turned to the waitress. "Then I'd like one of your chocolate milkshakes, a burger with everything, and the special fries."

"Your diet," Ethan whispered to Justin, and George smiled. "You have to start shooting next week."

"And he'll have the same," Justin said, nodding to Ethan, who looked as startled as a rabbit. "You're going to love it, and there isn't a lot of variety here like in LA. It's more basic."

The server looked at him a few times as though she was trying to work out who Justin was. George said nothing, figuring that it would be best if Justin could be himself for a few days instead of a movie star. If he wanted the attention, it would be easy enough to get it, George was sure. He placed his order, and their server left the table.

"Do you want to go to your dad's house after lunch?" George asked.

"I doubt there's anything there for me," Justin said.

"As far as I can tell, it hasn't changed much. The rooms are still the same." George remembered being surprised at how Mr. Grove had kept everything. He'd been in the house many times with Justin when they were teenagers, and when he'd showed up on his first home care appointment, it had been like walking back in time. Everything was in the same place, and he suspected that Justin's room was exactly the way he'd left it, but he couldn't be sure. The door to that room was always closed, and George had never peeked inside.

"I bet. Dad was always big on consistency. Never change anything unless you're forced to." Justin groaned. "Do you know if he tried to get in touch with me when my mother died? I found out months later when I ran into a cousin in California. She told me that Mom had cancer and they discovered it too late and she passed away a few months later."

George stared in total shock. "We all thought you didn't come back because of how things were with your dad. No one had any idea that he didn't—"

"No one told me. Maybe that's why he was feeling guilt now," Justin said.

"Come to the house. There have to be things there that belonged to your mother. You can take them back with you."

"I can't. None of it belongs to me," Justin said. "Whoever my dad left his shit to is going to get it all."

"Wait. Your dad never changed his will. He told me where it was and then showed it to me. Everything was left to you. The house, all of it." George remembered being surprised after the whole incident, but not half as shocked as Justin was at that moment.

Their server brought the food and set plates in front of each of them. Justin didn't seem to notice. Ethan, on the other hand, dug right in like he hadn't eaten in days. The guy was super skinny, so George figured he'd dieted for years and was finally getting a decent meal.

"Dang, this is good," Ethan said as he took his second bite of burger and then sucked his milkshake through the straw.

"He left everything to me?" Justin said. "There has to be some mistake."

"I don't think so," George said as he took a bite of one of his fries. "I think your father changed after your mother died. He still had his problems, but…."

"No," Justin argued. "Maybe my dad never got around to making another will, but the things he said and did couldn't be taken back or changed no matter what he might have wished." Justin shook his head. "Let's talk about something else. Is your mother still here?"

"Oh, yeah. She's a retired supervisor at the plant she worked at for years. She's still as gutsy and strong as ever." George grinned. "She wondered if you'd be coming back to town."

"Your mom was always a great lady."

"She would have taken you in," George said. "After what happened with your dad, she said you could come live with us." That got to the crux of the matter for him. "I went to find you, but you were gone. You called me from Harrisburg later that day and said you were on your way out of town." George glared at Justin. "We tried to help you, but you were already gone."

"I had to go," Justin said. "There were things I wanted to do that my father hated, and when he kicked me out I took it as a sign to get on with it. And I did. I worked my way across the country, and when I got to Hollywood, I met Ethan, who slapped me on the side of the head, literally."

You did?" George asked Ethan.

"Yeah. He was practically starving as he went from business to business trying to get a job. I put in a good word with the manager of this sleazy diner, and he started there. After that, it was one roller coaster after another. I had this really cheap place to live, a single room, and we lived there together for six months. This guy spent all his extra money on clothes and busted his feet going to every audition he could find, sometimes two or three a day." Ethan turned to Justin and then back to George. "You have nothing to fault him for. He arrived with nothing and worked like hell to get where he is." There was a tiger inside Ethan; that was for sure.

"So you made it big and you never looked back," George said to Justin.

"I worked hard and got lucky. But it's hard not to look back." Justin talked softly, and George noticed that a lot of heads were turned their way. "There are people I have missed since the day I left."

George didn't dare hope that he was one of them. His heart did a little leap anyway, and he looked down at the table and began eating once again.

"Mr. Hawthorne, would it be okay if I got your autograph?" a teenage girl asked as she came to stand next to the table. She held out a small notebook in shaking hands. George watched as Justin took it from her.

"Of course. What's your name?"

"Carrie," she answered softly, and Justin signed the autograph. "I heard you grew up here."

"Yes. I used to come into this diner with George here when he and I were about your age." He smiled at her as he handed back the book.

"I just love your movies," she told him, clutching the notebook like it was a precious object.

"Thank you. Are you still in high school?"

She nodded. "Tenth grade. I'm in the drama club, and we're trying to raise money for our winter production." She looked over toward a table and then back at Justin. "We're selling candy bars."

"How much are they?" Justin asked.

"Two dollars," she answered.

"Here." Justin pulled out his wallet and handed the girl a fifty-dollar bill. "I'll buy one, and you keep the change to help with the production, okay?" She took the bill and raced back to the table, then brought Justin his candy bar. "Thank you." He took it gently and shook her hand. Then the girl half floated back to her table, and Justin returned to his lunch as though nothing had happened.

"That was incredibly nice," George said.

"Justin is always nice," Ethan said. "He always has been. That was part of what attracted me and why I wanted to help him. If someone didn't look out for him, he was going to be chewed up and spat out by the sharks."

George nodded slowly. "Have you thought about where you're going to stay?"

"We stayed at a hotel last night, but we haven't given any thought beyond that. I wasn't sure what I was going to be walking into, so we didn't make any plans. If I had to, I figured we could go back to Baltimore, stay there, and fly home."

Obviously Justin hadn't been expecting any sort of welcome in his hometown. As much as George had wished for years that Justin had stayed with him, he had to admit that, at the time, there had been little here for him. Maybe leaving had been Justin's only choice. It seemed to have worked out for him, but it most definitely had left footprints on George's heart.

"Has there been anyone else?" George asked, no longer able to hold off asking what he really wanted to know. He wanted to know if Ethan and Justin were a couple. It was hard for him to tell by the way they acted. They were close; that was obvious. But Justin had introduced Ethan as a friend.

Justin leaned over the table, and a tingle of electricity went up George's back. He wanted him to lean far enough that George could meet him and find out if the way he kissed had changed or if his lips tasted the way he remembered. George swallowed, parting his lips slightly.

"If you're asking if Ethan and I are lovers, then no. We never have been. I've dated a little. But mostly I've worked and worked. Guys don't want someone who's on set for three months at a time."

George met Justin's piercing gaze. "I...."

Justin leaned closer. "They love the money and the bragging rights, and each and every one of them would like to be Mr. Hawthorne, but they don't really give a crap about me." The longing in Justin's voice was impossible to miss. "I'd like someone to like me for me, just once."

Justin sat back in his chair, and George did the same.

"What the hell happened?" George asked as anger rose in his gut.

Justin dug into his food, head down, and George turned to Ethan, hoping for an explanation. Ethan glanced at Justin and then shook his head. "You might as well tell him, or I will," Ethan chided, but Justin kept eating. "You saw him in *Lightning Strikes*, right?"

George nodded. "He was wonderful in that." He'd gone to the tiny local theater every night they had shown the movie just so he could see Justin in all his amazing, edible, shirt-off, glance-of-butt glory. The entire time Justin had been on-screen, George had been transfixed, and so had most everyone else in the theater.

"That role got him noticed by everyone and gave him his chance to catapult to stardom. It also got him noticed by a lot of guys."

"Do you really have to tell this story?" Justin asked and pushed Ethan until he let him out. He headed back toward the restrooms.

"He hates being reminded because he feels like a fool. Anyway, Leonard—Lenny—approached him on the set of his next picture, *Light of Stars*, and they started talking. Next thing they're going out together after shooting, and then Lenny's staying over at Justin's. He'd gotten a place of his own, and apparently Lenny had somehow moved himself in little by little. They were together all the time, and Justin was happy."

George braced for the bad news.

"The picture they were shooting together ended, and Justin had a bigger part in his next film. Lenny told him he should back out of the deal or pressure the director to find him a part in the film so they could work together again." Ethan set down his fork. "Justin was ready to do it. Thank God he talked to me. I told him he needed to get Lenny to back off a little and went back to his place to support Justin. We talked to him, and Lenny got angry and stormed out. The next day when Justin came home from shooting, he found Lenny in his bed with two guys, just to make Justin jealous. Justin kicked him out, and Lenny went *Fatal Attraction* on him. Justin's agent helped, and they got a restraining order. The parts for Lenny evaporated fast once word got around. Justin treats everyone well, from the directors to the caterers and makeup artists. They like him, and that goes a long way on the set."

"But those people don't decide who to hire," George said.

"Maybe not. But the community in Hollywood isn't that big, and everyone knows everyone else. The wardrobe people talk with the directors, and so do the heads of makeup. They get their face time, and if they don't like you, they mention it. Maybe not directly, but they say things like 'so-and-so's skin is getting bad, and it takes so much makeup and time to make him look good.' The wardrobe people complain that it takes extra time to maintain his clothes, all those kinds of things. If a director hears complaints from every quarter, then maybe that actor gets branded as hard to work with. And that equals more money, because everything in Hollywood costs money. But Justin is loved, so everyone closed ranks around him."

"Did he come out because of that?"

Ethan shook his head. "Justin never hid who he was. He was strong that way. His agent is good, and when he said he wasn't going to hide, Roy made the most of it. Gay audiences applauded his bravery, and from there his work spoke for itself."

Justin returned from the bathroom, and Ethan let him slide back into his seat as murmurs raced through the room. "I love how I can sit here for an hour, but the minute I go to the restroom, they start buzzing," Justin said. "Makes me want to yell, 'Yes, I do pee.'"

George had taken a drink of his water, and it was all he could do not to spray it everywhere.

"Did he finish the story?" Justin asked.

George swallowed hard and nodded. "You have nothing to be ashamed of."

"Ethan told me to watch out, and I didn't believe him. After that I asked Ethan to move into the house with me. Officially he's my private secretary and helps keep me organized. Mostly he looks after me and helps make sure I'm where I'm supposed to be. He's also my voice of caution and reason. But he's not my boyfriend."

"Justin's not my type," Ethan chimed in, and George rolled his eyes. He found it hard to understand why Justin wouldn't be anyone and everyone's type.

"I asked about your mom, but you didn't say anything about your dad. Is he still making furniture?" Justin asked. "Mr. Miller makes the most incredible pieces," he told Ethan. "He sells them all over the country. Maybe while we're here I could meet with him and we could arrange for him to do some pieces for the house?"

"Justin, my dad passed away two years ago," George said. "I didn't know how to get in touch with you directly or I would have called. I did try, but there were so many people, and I didn't know how to get past them."

"Georgie," Justin said, his voice breaking.

George's eyes filled with tears, and he did his best to push them away. He hated when this happened. He could be fine for months, and then something would happen and the ache of missing his dad would come rushing back. Justin pushed past Ethan and slid onto the bench seat next to George, and then he put his arm around George's shoulders.

"I missed him more than my own dad when I left," Justin whispered into his ear and tightened his hold.

George came back to himself pretty quickly. He'd had time to accept his dad's passing. He realized that Justin was quietly crying on his shoulder. George wasn't sure if it was for his dad or Justin's. Maybe it was a jumble of emotions and the loss of both had gotten mixed together.

"It's all right."

"What happened?" Justin muttered.

"He had a massive heart attack in his shop. He was working to get an order done, and when he didn't come in, Mama got worried. She called me, and together we went out and found him on the floor. Machines still running. There was nothing we could do. I called an ambulance, but he was already dead and had been for a few hours by then." George rubbed the moisture from his eyes. "He went happy, doing what he loved. It was hard on Mama for a long time, but she's starting to move on with her life."

Justin nodded and pulled his head away from George's shoulder. His eyes were puffy and his nose red. Ethan handed him a napkin, and Justin wiped his eyes and nose before sitting up straight in the booth. Ethan slid Justin's plate across the table so he could finish eating.

"If you don't want to stay at a hotel, I have room at my house. You could stay there if you want," George offered. "Of course, you could also stay at your dad's."

"No. I'll never stay there again," Justin said quickly. "That place is nothing to me. It stopped being my home seven years ago." He began eating again. "It stopped being anything to me when my dad kicked me out and my mother did nothing to stop him. I reached out to her a few months later, and she said she'd be in touch, but I think my dad found out because it never happened. At least that's what I thought. I now know that she died and the old bastard didn't bother to tell me."

"Okay. Then you can stay at my house if you like. It's a mile or so out of town, toward Gettysburg, and no one should bother you there. That is, unless you'd rather go back to the hotel."

Justin and Ethan shared a look. "That would be very nice. Thank you," Justin answered. "Are you sure there's room for both of us? We don't want to be a bother." They had checked out of the hotel, figuring they'd need to have a flexible schedule and not knowing how long they'd stay.

"There's room."

"Don't you have to work?"

"I have another client I'm scheduled to take starting on Monday. Her daughter is caring for her now. So I have the week off, so to speak. They'll call if I need to back up any of the other nurses, but otherwise...."

"Then thank you. I hate hotels, and I spend way too much time in them."

Justin's expression let go of some of the hurt, and George went back to his lunch. Justin ate as well, and Ethan finished his plate and sucked the last of his milkshake through his straw.

"Would you like some pie for dessert?" the server asked when she returned to the table.

Justin asked what kind they had and ordered a slice of apple for each of them.

Ethan protested until he took one bite and then inhaled his piece like a vacuum cleaner. "After two days here, I'm going to have to go on a diet for six months."

"Complain all you want," Justin said as he took a bite of his own, "but you're eating like a horse."

"Maybe, but I'm not the one who will have to be seen in front of the camera in a week." Ethan glared at Justin for two seconds and then returned to eating. Once Ethan had eaten his last bite, he got up and went to the back, toward the restrooms.

"He seems like a good friend," George said, trying to dispel the stab of jealousy he knew he had no right to have.

"Ethan is an amazing friend. He always tells me the truth, even when I don't want to hear it. People in Hollywood are masters at blowing smoke up your ass and telling you exactly what you want to hear rather than giving an honest opinion. Sometimes you need to hear when you're full of shit." Justin took another bite and then turned toward him.

Instantly George felt the current between them, just like he had in high school algebra class. Back then he always knew where Justin was and when he was looking at him. George had always felt it. He was being stupid; he knew it. Maybe what he felt was only some holdover from what they'd meant to each other then, or wishful thinking. "You know, you have friends here too. Just because your father turned his back doesn't mean everyone else did."

Justin took a deep breath. "I had to get away and try for my dream. You know that."

"So you would have left anyway, eventually?" George asked. "Regardless of what happened, you were going to leave me." That hurt.

"I don't know what I would have done if things had been different. But they weren't. My home was ripped away, and I had a chance to try for a whole new life. The people who should have loved me most turned their backs, so why wouldn't everyone else? I left, went out West, rolled the dice, and I came up a winner."

"Did you really?" George asked, letting his gaze bore into Justin until he turned away.

Justin's fork jangled when he set it on the plate. Their server had placed the check on the edge of the table, and Justin grabbed it and got up, going to the register.

"That isn't necessary," George said, but there was only Ethan to hear it.

"He's going to need some time," Ethan told him.

"I don't understand."

"I think you do. He's rediscovering something he thought was lost to him, and from what I've heard, you're part of that." Ethan shifted to get comfortable on the lumpy seat.

"You really care for him?"

Ethan chuckled. "He's the brother I wish I had. I'm not his lover, and I never will be, but we need each other. We're a family of two that we made for ourselves."

"Would you say that if he wasn't a huge success?" George asked.

Ethan's gaze grew cold as ice. "I was his friend when he had nothing after his father kicked him out and his confidence was shot to hell. So you don't get to ask questions like that. Yes, he pays for things for me and I live in his house, but I also go where he goes and make sure he's okay." Ethan leaned over the table, the intensity in his expression not softening one iota. "Do you understand? If anyone wants to get to him, they have to go through me or over my dead body."

"You're serious," George observed.

"He's my family." Ethan sat back in the booth. "Justin is strong—very strong—and smart, but he carries the scars of what happened. Don't let the confident exterior fool you. I picked up the pieces of what happened here, and while he's never said a word, I know there's more to it than just his father."

George swallowed hard. "Excuse me?"

Ethan nodded. "Something else happened after his dad kicked him out. He doesn't talk about it, but something scared the crap out of him and gave his feet wings that sent him West." He turned toward the register. "I'm only telling you this because I don't know anyone in town, and I'm hoping for the sake of your old friendship that you'll help him exorcise whatever demon has been hounding him."

George tried to think of anything that had happened around the time that Justin left town. Justin came back to the table, and Ethan stood, staying next to him. George saw him looking around the restaurant, and then he leaned in, whispering something, and Justin walked to a table back by the window.

George got out of the booth and turned to watch as Justin knelt by a little boy in a wheelchair. "That's Bobby Masten. He's been in a chair all his life."

George watched as Justin and Bobby laughed together, and when Bobby turned to him, Justin gave the slight boy a hug that earned a smile bright enough to light the entire room. Ethan hurried over and handed Justin a card before standing next to him once again.

"Are those pictures or something?"

"No, just blank cards. But this way he has something to sign that's better than a napkin."

George watched Justin with Bobby, unable to take his eyes off him. Others moved closer, but Justin kept his attention on Bobby, making him feel special. Then Justin stood, grinned, and headed grinned and headed right for the door. George and Ethan followed him out.

"Always know when to make an exit," Justin explained with a grin. "The vultures were beginning to circle."

"What does that mean?" George asked.

Justin reached his car—a rental, George figured by the stickers—and pulled open the door. "That everyone in the diner was trying to figure out if now was the time that they could approach and ask for an autograph. I like to give them, but on my own terms. Being mobbed isn't my favorite thing."

"I suppose it isn't," George said. "My car is right over there, and we're just a mile or so from the house. Turn around and come up behind me, and I'll lead the way."

"Thanks, Georgie," Justin said and got into the car.

George hurried across PA 34 and unlocked his car. It was old and partly held together with duct tape. But Bert had many miles left in him, and that was all that mattered. The dents and dings were superficial, but the engine would last forever. He slid into the worn driver's seat and pulled into nonexistent traffic. George passed Justin and Ethan, watching in his rearview mirror as they fell in behind.

They followed as he made the easy trip that involved only two turns, and then he pulled into his driveway. During the entire trip George tried to slow his racing heart. Every time Justin called him Georgie, he flashed back to the ease and attraction they'd had between them years ago.

George's mother came out to meet him, and she squealed with delight and rushed down the drive when she saw Justin. "I'm so glad you're here."

By the time George had closed his door and turned around, his mother had Justin in a tight hug and was rocking him back and forth.

"I'm so angry with you, and I missed you so much. I don't know whether to hug you or swat your behind." To George's delight, she released Justin from her grip, swatted him, and then hugged him once again. "Come on inside." She turned to Ethan. "Is this your boyfriend?"

35

"Ethan is my best friend," Justin said. "This is George's mother," he added, introducing her to Ethan.

"Call me Shirley, both of you, and get inside."

She let go of Justin and hugged Ethan, who didn't seem to know what to do in the face of George's mama. Then she turned to him. George hugged his mother and kissed her on the cheek.

"As you can see, I ran into an old friend this morning." He grinned.

"He did get to see his father before he passed? I had hoped he would." His mother was pleased. "That doctor owed me a favor."

George lowered his gaze, turning to see where Justin and Ethan were. "You didn't."

"Of course I did," she said softly. "I went to see the old coot, and he told me to try to call Justin, so I made sure the doctor heard and convinced him to call. They both needed some peace, and this was the only way to get it." She smiled to herself. "Besides, it got him back here." She winked at him.

"I know you thought a lot of Justin, but he has a different life now, and we're different people. So don't push. You have to promise to leave things alone." He met her gaze and refused to look away.

"All right. But at least tell me he isn't dating the man with him."

"He and Ethan are like brothers, and no, Justin isn't seeing anyone." His mother could be such a small-town busybody. There were times when he really wished she would let things happen on their own. "But that doesn't mean anything. He's only here for a few days, and then he's going back to his life. He starts shooting another movie on Monday."

"A lot can happen in that time," his mother said.

"A funeral, remember? That isn't the background of joy one hopes to have when you rekindle a romance." He rolled his eyes. "Just let things be. I'm glad I got to see him again, and that's enough for me." George knew it would have to be enough. The world-famous Justin Hawthorne was not going to stay in Biglerville, Pennsylvania, for very long, and the feelings they'd had for each other all those years ago weren't going to suddenly burst back into bloom. George was a realist, and he didn't believe in love at first sight or anything like that. Justin's return was some sort of miracle, and he'd make the most of the time he had with his friend. But he had no illusions that in a few days, once Justin's dad's funeral was over, Justin and Ethan wouldn't get on a plane and fly back to the other side of the country.

His mother nodded, and George wasn't sure if she'd leave things alone or not. He shot her a final warning look and then went inside.

Justin and Ethan stood in the living room waiting for him. "I recognize these pieces," Justin told him. "They're your dad's."

"Yeah, some of them. I made the coffee table," George said. "Dad was finishing a large commission when he passed. It took a while, but it was nearly done, so I finished it and delivered the pieces. He and I had worked together enough that I was able to do it." George tried to look at the tables and built-in bookcase the way Justin did. "I've done what I can to take after my dad. But only as a hobby." He motioned down the hall. "I thought Justin could stay in here, and Ethan, I can put you in this room. It also serves as an office of sorts." He opened the doors.

"That's very nice of you, Georgie," Justin said. "I really appreciate it." He went into the room and closed the door.

George turned to Ethan, hoping for an explanation, but Ethan seemed confused as well.

"I'm going to get the luggage from the trunk."

He went back through the house, and George figured he could put some coffee and tea on. It would give him something to do while they settled in.

The television sounded as he ran the water, his mother trying to find her channel. She was addicted to soap operas and had been for decades. She had to watch her stories and very seldom missed them. So George was surprised when the big, expansive music sounded. Once he got the kettle on, he peered into the other room and found his mother watching a DVD of *Light of Stars*.

"Real subtle, Mother," George chided.

"I haven't seen it," she said innocently.

George leaned closer. "You just want to see Justin's bare butt," he told her.

She turned to him as if scandalized and then went back to the movie. "I may be old, but I'm not dead."

She sat back, and George helped Ethan with the bags when he came inside.

"Is this it?" George said hopefully as he took the largest bag.

"Yes. That's Justin's, and so is this one." Ethan set down the other large bag. George hoisted it and followed Ethan down the hall, where he knocked on Justin's door. When he got an answer, he went inside with the bags and closed the door.

"You didn't tell me your house was the one you grew up in," Justin scolded.

"After Dad died, I bought it from Mom, and we added on a bedroom and sitting room for her. It gave us both some privacy. Why does it matter?" George asked, sitting next to Justin on the bed.

"This was your room," Justin whispered and turned to him. "Do you remember what happened in this room?"

Justin bounced slightly, and George's eyes widened. *Good God—he did remember.*

"Your mom and dad had left to go to a show in Harrisburg, and the two of us started out playing video games, and we ended up in this room… in bed together."

Justin swallowed, and George watched his throat work, longing to lean closer and kiss it to see if Justin still tasted as strong and rich as he remembered.

"You never forget your first time," George said. "It was like an entire world opened up to me in an afternoon." Justin's hand rested close to his on the bed, and George wanted to place his hand on top. Hell, he was tempted to ask if a re-creation of that afternoon was possible. "I learned so much about myself and about you in those few hours."

"Yeah. It seems like a lifetime ago." Justin blinked. "Has there been anyone special in your life? Please tell me there has."

"Yeah. I met someone about two and a half years ago at a club in Harrisburg. He was really cute, smaller than me, and bright as they come. I'd only stopped in at Bronco's to have a drink with some friends when I saw him dancing. He moved like sex on wheels, and when he saw me watching him, he came over and asked me to dance." George made a face.

"You don't dance?" Justin asked.

"I'm like a dying chicken, and I usually hurt the people around me, but he pulled me onto the floor, and after watching him, I tried to mimic his moves. He seemed happy with what he saw and moved closer. Soon we were dancing, and then kissing…. It was nice. Afterward, he asked for my number, and we dated for a few months. But he was a club kid. It was what he loved. I wasn't interested in going out every weekend. I did for a while, but it got to be the same thing with the same people, having the same conversation time after time about who was with whom or some piece of overblown drama that meant nothing but was talked about for months."

Justin nodded. "My luck hasn't been much better, as Ethan told you. Now I pretty much keep to myself in that department."

"Why?" George asked expectantly.

"Who am I going to date? Straight actors date actresses, and you see how well that turns out. They fall in love and break up on the pages of *People* magazine. How depressing is that? I don't want my private life to be something open for public consumption. I really think that there is too much pressure on two actors for most relationships."

"Why?" George asked.

Justin turned on the bed to face him. "Next week I start shooting on my next picture. I'll be at the studio by four or five in the morning for makeup and wardrobe, then on set for much of the day. In the evening, the director will watch the day's take and make sure he got what he needed, and I'll be working through the scenes and lines for the next day. I might get home about ten or eleven only to start the day all over again. There is little time to spend with someone else. Sometimes I don't even have time to make a phone call. And that's if we're in the studio. On-location shooting is more demanding because of all the travel expenses involved. Everyone is working even harder, because once the light is gone, it's done for the day, and time is always money."

"Are you saying that acting couples don't love each other?" George asked.

"No, I think they do, but the nature of the business tears them apart. A lot of relationships start when they meet on set. They get close during a movie production when they're together all the time, but they can't sustain the separation of different productions going on into the future forever. Sometimes one of the people gives up their career for the other, but I can imagine resentment creeps in."

"So it sounds to me as though you expect to spend the rest of your life alone," George commented. "That sounds like a lonely life to me."

"It's better than having your heart ripped apart all the time." Justin sighed. "I know I sound like I'm whining, and I don't mean to. I love my work and I'm good at it. But I also know the pitfalls, so I cultivate my image, and if I do have a relationship again—and for the record, I really hope to—I want to be careful enough and have a chance to get to know the person as me. That's pretty hard, though, because most people know Justin Hawthorne, and I keep hoping that someone will be able to look past that and find Justin Grove. It hasn't happened up until now, and I don't know if it will."

George opened his mouth to say he already saw Justin Grove, and he'd always known who that man was. He knew what it meant when Justin wrung his hands on his lap the way he was doing now. He knew the nervous energy that was building up and that it had to come out. He also knew the kind, gentle man underneath the façade of the famous Mr. Hawthorne. That part of him had come out for a few minutes at the diner when he'd been talking to Bobby. That was the man George knew and would always look for. But it didn't matter, not any longer. That person was lost to him and had been since Justin left town. Maybe things would be different if Justin was here to stay, but he wasn't. Justin was here for a few days, and then he was going back to his life in Hollywood, and there was no reason for George to make any more of things than that. The result would only be another round of heartache that would take months to get over, and he couldn't go through that all over again. The first time had been gut-wrenching. "I should let you unpack and get comfortable. I'll put out some towels and things for you and Ethan in the bathroom across the hall."

"Thanks, Georgie. I really appreciate you doing this."

Justin took George's hand, squeezing it gently. George swallowed a gasp at the burst of heat and energy that sang its way up his arm. He clenched his fingers, holding on to Justin as long as he dared, not wanting the connection, as fragile as it was, to break. He dared not close his eyes or even move for fear that any movement would shatter the moment. He'd never considered that something as innocent as holding hands could send waves of memories that unleashed pent-up longing and wishes he never thought would see the light of day again.

And yet it was George who pulled his hand away first. He had to get out of the room before he did something stupid. "You're always welcome here. You always were," he said and left the room. Ethan's door was open, and humming flowed into the hallway as he unpacked.

"Is it okay if I plug in my computer?" Ethan asked as he stuck his head out into the hall.

"Sure. Let me get you the Wi-Fi password, and you can do what you need to." George went into the room and got the card out of the drawer, then handed it to Ethan. "I have to ask what we should do if people start to show up."

"You mean like fans?" Ethan asked.

"Or reporters. People have seen him in town. They may call the papers or something."

"If fans show up, we'll tell them that Justin is here to attend his father's funeral and ask them to give him some space to breathe and grieve. That should get us what we need. If reporters make an appearance, I'll tell them the same thing. Local people are more sensitive than the tabloids usually are."

"All right," George agreed.

"And if someone tries to get too close, call the police and report them. Sending a reporter who gets too aggressive to jail is fine. They need to know the limits. It's something we've done before."

"You have?"

"Yeah. We had one guy who climbed the fence and was trying to put a ladder up to Justin's bedroom window in order to get pictures of him. He went to jail for almost a year. But what scared him most was when the security guys held him at gunpoint. He pissed himself good." Ethan chuckled.

"You really have to put up with things like that? I thought those were just television plots or something."

"I wish they were. Justin gets his picture taken almost everywhere he goes. We keep the house a safe place, and the security service sweeps it every few weeks in case a workman or the pool service tries to get a listening device inside."

George's chin practically hit the floor. "You're kidding!"

"Nope. It happened last year. They only got as far as the pool house, but there was a listening device. We could never prove who placed it, but we try to be safe and do our best to provide some privacy for him."

"How can he stand it?" George asked.

"It's the price you pay for fame. Justin is an amazing actor, but that kind of life comes with costs, a lot of them. Most people don't realize that until it's too late."

Ethan turned and smiled. George followed his gaze. Damn, Justin looked amazing leaning on the doorframe, relaxed, arms lightly folded over his chest, eyes soft and gentle, the way George remembered them when they'd been alone at the creek on a particular Saturday afternoon. Heat rose, and he knew his face had to be growing red.

George excused himself quickly and left the room, going to sit on the sofa next to his mother. He arrived just in time to see Justin's character step toward the bed, flashing a hint of butt for just a second. More than once he'd paused the DVD and gone frame by frame so he could get a look at it. Hell, more than once in his room, he'd.... George put that out of his mind and closed his eyes, remembering where he was. It was never good to get a stiffy in public, and certainly not in front of his mother. That thought was enough to have his balls crawling back into his body.

"What are you going to do this afternoon?" his mother asked, pausing the DVD long enough to get up and bring in a pot of tea and some cups on a tray, which she placed on the coffee table.

George sighed and brought his mind back where it was supposed to be. "I don't know. I have my key to Justin's dad's house, so I was going to see if Justin wanted to go over and look at things. It's his now, after all, and he's going to need to make some decisions."

"Sell it all," Justin said as he came into the room. "The house and everything in it."

George said nothing, trying to get a handle on an argument he could use to reason with him.

His mother dove right in. "Justin Grove, you aren't too big to put over my knee. Now sit down right there. Just because you are old enough to flash that behind I used to change when you were in diapers, that doesn't mean I won't do it." The snap in her voice had Justin jumping, just the way it always had. "Things were crap between you and your father. I know that. But that was your mother's house as well, and she loved you no matter what. It hurt her no end what your father did, but she was old-fashioned, you know that, and she couldn't stand up to your father. I know she wished she had, but by then it was too late and she got sick." She poured cups of tea and handed one to Justin, who took it automatically.

"There's nothing there for me. Just sell it all, and I'll donate the proceeds to the American Cancer Society. That way it will do someone some good."

"Justin…," Mom warned. "Go over and see the house. You don't have to take anything you don't want. George and I will see to it that your wishes are carried out. But give yourself a chance to heal. This will stay with you if you let it."

"She's right," Ethan said, entering the room and taking a cup as well.

When Justin turned toward Ethan, the look he gave him was the stare of death. It left George cold from across the room, but Ethan stared right back.

"Don't give me that look. I know what it is, and so help me, I'll slap it off your pretty face." Ethan turned to George's mother. "Give us an hour."

"I'm not going," Justin said and set down his untouched cup.

"Fine, then George and I will go, and I'll arrange for a company to come in, pack every single thing, and ship it to the house in LA. And when it arrives, you'll be on set and I'll have all of it piled in your bedroom. Floor to ceiling. You'll have to wade through it to go to bed."

Man, Ethan had brass balls. "You wouldn't dare," Justin growled.

"Try me," Ethan said. "All that unpleasantness can be avoided if you come with George and me in an hour. That should be enough time for you to gird your loins or whatever it is you do before you have to perform a gut-wrenching scene, man up, and deal with your parents." Ethan turned to him. "Do you know who the executor of the estate is?"

"You're looking at her," Mom said, and Ethan sat back, laughing.

"Ass," Justin swore at him.

"You have an hour. Do you need to make some phone calls? I bet Roy is shitting bricks about now."

"Yes, I'm sure he is, and you really are an ass." Justin stood and stalked off toward the bedroom, and Ethan looked exceedingly pleased with himself.

"That boy hasn't changed much. He's still as stubborn as the mule that kicked him when he was seven and determined to try and ride it."

Ethan leaned forward. "Excuse me?" He sounded delighted. "Stories about Justin?" He rubbed his hands together like an evil pixie. "I'm all ears."

Mom howled and launched into a story about George and Justin as kids, and how they'd decided to visit the farm down the road. George knew the story because his mother told it to everyone, so he wandered down the hall. Justin's door was open, and he was on the phone, pacing the floor.

"I'm fine. No one has tried to kidnap me or even looked at me cross-eyed. Will you stop worrying? I'm staying with old friends, and they'll protect me from the boogeymen." Justin kept pacing. "Yes, I read the contract and it's fine, but I'm not going to sign it until I get the script. E-mail it to Ethan and I'll read it over."

Justin stopped pacing and sat on the edge of the bed. George could hear the roughness in the voice coming through the line.

"Roy!" Justin snapped. "I know you read it over, but you also said that sci-fi epic would be a great fit for me. It was a disaster, if you remember. Thank God I turned it down and sidestepped that pile of shit you wanted me to wade into." Jesus Christ, Justin was a real ballbuster. "Now send me the script, and if I like it, I'll take the part." He was clearly getting upset. "Of course I know it's top secret. No, like I was thinking of plastering the pages all over town." He listened some more. "Thank you." He pulled the phone away from his ear and called out, "Ethan, you're being sent a script." He went back to talking to Roy.

"Got it," Ethan said, and Justin relayed the message. "I sent it to your tablet so you can read it there."

George leaned against the doorframe.

"Thank you," Justin said into the phone. "I have it. I'll read it over as soon as I can. This afternoon I'm going to my father's house so I can see what he left me. I've decided I'll sell most of it and donate the proceeds to the ACS. My mother died of cancer." Justin stood once again and began pacing. "I'll be back in time to shoot on Monday. I'm in the studio, so it should be fine." Justin walked faster. "When was the last time I missed anything? Hell, can you remember the last time I was late for anything at all? Just back off and let me get through all this." He suddenly sounded ragged, and the man in charge wavered.

Instantly George remembered the day Justin had come to his house, sporting a black eye and carrying a suitcase. George had hidden Justin in his room while he cried his eyes out, the gut-wrenching pain twisting at his stomach. Justin was rarely fragile, but he had been as brittle as the most delicate glass that night. They'd slept in the same

45

bed, and he'd held Justin for hours. George had told Justin that he loved him and would never let him go, no matter what.

"Georgie, I love you too," Justin had said, and eventually they'd slept.

George had wanted to help, and the following morning while Justin was supposedly at work, he'd told his mom and dad what had happened. They'd been more than willing to offer Justin a home, but he never came back. Now, as he heard that fragile tone again, he wondered if Ethan was right. Something else… something… more must have happened to drive Justin out of town.

"I'll be back in plenty of time," Justin said, pulling George out of his thoughts. George stood up straight and left the doorway. He hadn't meant to listen in on Justin's call, and he was embarrassed he'd done so.

"Georgie," Justin called as he appeared in the doorway. "Was there something you needed?"

George shook his head. How was he supposed to explain that he'd somehow felt Justin might need him and he'd just walked down the hallway to where he was? It seemed stupid to his own ears, let alone saying it out loud. "Finish up what you need to, and we'll go when you're ready." He turned and went back to the living room.

CHAPTER 3

ETHAN DROVE and George navigated while Justin sat in the backseat of the rental car, arms folded over his chest. He was none too happy about this whole idea, but they'd goaded and guilted him into it.

"The funeral home called, and they have taken the body and are preparing it. The local minister called as well, and he wants to come by on Tuesday to speak with you about the service," George said.

Justin said nothing. He had no preference about anything. He could hardly believe it was Sunday and that so much had changed about his life in a matter of two days.

"Go back toward where we had lunch and turn left at the light in the center of town. The house is just a block off the main road."

George turned to look at him. Justin turned away, partly out of annoyance and partly because he didn't need to encourage the feelings that kept bubbling up from inside.

The house looked the same as they pulled up to the front. Well, pretty much the same. It had been painted at some point, and the trim was darker, but otherwise it looked almost exactly as it had the day he'd left. There was no use arguing. He was here, so he might as well make the most of it. "Let's get this over with." The street was quiet and the sun was bright, even if it was cool. Justin knew from experience that it would get quite cold once the sun went down.

George unlocked the door, and Justin stepped back into the house he honestly never thought he'd see again. It looked very much the same. His mother's sofa was in the same place on the same worn carpet Justin had played on as a kid. The tables hadn't been changed, and even the pictures and decorations on the walls were the same. The chair that had always been his father's had been replaced, but that was about all.

Justin continued through the house. The kitchen was like going back in time, and he pulled one of the chairs out from under the table and sat down in the place that had been his. For a second he could hear his mother at the stove, humming to herself. That lasted mere seconds, and then Justin stood, nearly toppling the chair in his haste. He walked down the hall and pushed open the door to his old room.

"It's like a time machine," he said quietly. The bed was still in the same place with his spread on it. It was covered in dust, and Justin wondered how long it had been since anyone had been in there. He guessed that his mother had been the last to clean inside. His things were still on the dresser, and when he pulled open the drawers, he saw they were empty, as was the closet. His mother had probably cleared out his clothes, but the rest was like it had always been.

"Is there anything in here you'd like to take with you?" George asked.

Justin shook his head. He'd left all this behind and hadn't thought about it in years. The desk under the window caught his attention. Justin pulled open one of the drawers and smiled. "Oh my God," he whispered as he pulled out an old scrapbook his mother had started for him. He set it on the bed and continued digging, coming up with some framed pictures. "Look at us." He wiped his fingers over the glass.

He and George smiled out of the frame, arms around each other's shoulders. They were shirtless, wet, and standing on a dock.

"I remember that. It was at Pinchot Park," George said. "We'd been swimming, and your mom took the picture." George handed it back. "You pushed me in right after she snapped the shutter."

Justin placed the picture on top of the album and went through the other drawers. He found old hobby things that were long past usable, pens, paper, and other bits that had been important once.

"What's across the hall?"

"The bathroom," Justin answered and went to the next room, opening the door to his mother's sewing room.

The machine was still there, but the mounds of fabric and thread were gone. To his disappointment, there was very little left of his mother in the room. He'd been hoping to find something of her. The closet was empty, and Justin left, then went to open the door to the master bedroom.

The room was dominated by the bed and medical equipment. "Georgie, are there people who can use all this?"

"Yes."

"Then take it to the agency you work for so it gets to those who need it." He went right to the dresser that had been his mother's and pulled out the top drawer. That had been the one she'd kept her stuff in, and it was full. The others had been cleaned out, but that one seemed untouched. Justin pulled it all the way out and dumped it on the bed before going through it.

Mostly the drawer contained bits of junk that he tossed in the trash as he went. There were a few boxes that he set aside until he found a small ring box. Justin opened it, smiled, and closed the box again, holding it tight. "I gave this to her for her fortieth birthday. I was sixteen, and I'd seen her eyeing it in the jeweler's window, so I saved up my money from my jobs and bought it for her. I'd heard her and Dad fighting about it because she'd said that was what she'd wanted and he'd been too cheap to get it. I figured he'd have gotten rid of it by now."

"Is there anything else you want?" George asked.

He finished picking through what was left and placed anything good that he didn't want back in the drawer. The rest he tossed. "No. There's nothing else here for me." What surprised Justin was how cold and lifeless the house felt. He'd expected and braced himself for a rush of emotion that hadn't happened. Maybe too much time had passed.

Justin gathered up the few things he'd found and carried them to the living room. He sat on the sofa and scanned the room again. Things were much as they'd always been, but they held nothing for him. This was the room where his father had yelled at him and, in the end, disowned him and thrown him out of their lives. Justin's mother had been in the kitchen, and he liked to think that she'd cried when he left, but she certainly never stood up to his father about it.

"I wondered…," George said as he sat down next to him. "I don't think your dad expected you to go, not really."

"Doesn't matter now. I did leave. He threw me out, and now they're both dead. So any explanations or excuses are gone with them." Justin was empty, or at least he felt that way. He knew he should feel something, anything, but he was calm, sitting in the house he grew up in, a place he never thought he'd see again, and he didn't really care. He wondered if he should yell or scream, maybe let anger tear the place up, but no, all he got was a huge pile of nothing. "Maybe we should go."

"All right," George said. "But there's one more thing I think you should see."

George patted him on the shoulder, and Justin stood and followed George out to the garage. He opened the door and stepped aside, turning on the light. Justin took a single step into the space, and his eyes bugged out of his head.

"Your dad got it a few years ago, and he spent all his spare time on it," George said. "He went to shows to get parts and even mixed the paint himself in order to match the exact red of the '64 Corvette."

"Oh my God," Justin muttered. "It's beautiful."

"Before he got sick, I'd sometimes see him out here working on it. But I never stopped to talk about it because I hated him for what he'd done. Then, when I was assigned to him, he took me out here, handed me the keys, and asked me to drive it a little every few weeks in order to keep the car in top condition. Up until a few weeks ago, he thought he'd get strong enough to get back to driving it, and after that, he kept talking about what he wanted done with things."

"And the car?" Justin asked curiously.

"He never said a word."

"Figures," Justin said quietly. "I bet he thought he'd changed his will years ago, so it didn't matter."

George shook his head. "He knew he hadn't and who was named. He told me a week before he died. Your dad said he hoped you'd come back."

"I don't understand," Justin said as he approached the car with its white scoops on the side and black top.

"Your dad put hours, months, of work into this car, yet he only drove it to keep it in good condition. He didn't take it to car shows, though he could have with Carlisle just a few miles away. This car was your dad's baby, and he never did anything with it, and he didn't change his will."

"So you're saying that he knew this would come to me?" Justin asked, turning away from the red and white leather interior as George went inside and returned with the keys. He set them in Justin's hand, but Justin could only stare at them. Well, not the keys so much as the ring they were on. It was a stupid plastic key ring that held pictures. What shocked him was his face staring out at him. He had to have been in the first or second grade, smiling with no front teeth. When he turned it over, he nearly dropped the ring. It was a picture of him in high school. He looked so young.

"I'm saying I think he did this for you."

"Why?" Justin asked.

"I don't know. Your dad was very closed off. I saw him every day, and he rarely talked about anything other than how he was feeling. Even then, most of the time, it was only so I could do my job. But when he was in pain from the stroke complications and had to take the strong medication, he'd sometimes open up, and I got the picture that your dad was a lonely, regretful man. Those times he'd talk about you as a child and how you used to put on plays by hanging a curtain across the hallway."

"There are probably still marks in the plaster."

"I think he knew he'd messed up badly." George snapped his fingers as if remembering something and hurried back to the house.

Justin opened the car door and slid into the driver's seat. The leather accommodated him incredibly, and he smiled at the relative simplicity and elegance of the interior.

"I'll arrange to have the car shipped to LA," Ethan said as he leaned inside, and all Justin could do was nod.

51

"I saw your dad working on this a few times, but he always hid it when I was around."

George held what looked like one of Justin's mother's scrapbooks. Justin got out of the car and closed the door with a thud that echoed off the garage walls. He handed Ethan the keys and followed George back inside. They went through to the living room.

"Your dad guarded this like it was the Holy Grail. He never let me look inside. He kept it next to his bed when he was sick, and I thought it was pictures of your mother." George placed the book on his lap. "I think your mother started it, and then your dad continued it after she died."

Justin opened the book and paged through it. There were clippings from the paper about him and his early roles, photos of him in costume, theater ticket stubs, printed pictures from the Internet, pages of *People* magazine, and even the magazine covers he'd done. It was all there, his career and life between the pages of a book. "I don't understand."

"I didn't either when I saw it. Like I said, your dad guarded it, but a few times when he was on the medication, he'd ask for it and page through. I'm convinced that what he did to you was his greatest regret, and he didn't know how to say he was sorry."

"All he had to do was pick up the fucking phone. He didn't even bother to call me when my mom died." He slammed the book closed. "The asshole was too selfish to let me know she was gone. And you say that he didn't know how to say he was *sorry*? That's bullshit! My father may have regretted his decisions, but he didn't regret them enough to make amends for them." Justin got to his feet. "Let's get the hell out of here."

"Justin—" George began.

Justin cut him off. "The old guy is dead. He may have felt remorse and been sorry, but I don't accept his apology. He tore me up inside and made me feel worthless. He took away the family that should have loved me no matter what. All for his precious ego. And as for the fucker not knowing how to say he was sorry, it's easy." Justin picked up the phone. "I'm sorry I was such an asshole!" he screamed into it at the top of his lungs and then slammed it back down. "See? It's fucking easy. There's nothing the hell to it."

Justin needed air, and he needed out of this place. He stepped around the coffee table and walked to the front door, tore it open, and hurried out into the front yard. Once outside, he gulped in air, filling his lungs and emptying them to do it again. His tunneled vision slowly began to expand once again, and he closed his eyes to try to still the swimming in his head. This whole thing was a bad idea. He never should have allowed them to talk him into coming here. It was stupid.

After a few minutes, he heard the front door open and close. He turned his head to see Ethan carrying a box to the car. He opened the trunk and set it inside. "What are you doing?"

"Taking care of things. George is locking up, and we'll be ready to go in a few minutes."

Ethan closed the trunk while Justin tried to calm his racing heart and keep complete embarrassment from taking over. He shouldn't have yelled like that. What happened wasn't their fault, but he hadn't been able to hold it in any longer. The door closed with a deep thud, and Justin felt footsteps behind him.

"I didn't mean to upset you," George said in a whisper.

"It wasn't your fault," Justin said.

"The house is locked, and we can get out of here."

Justin nodded and turned around. "Sell it all, including the house. Ethan will arrange to ship the car, and everything else can be sold or given to charity. I don't want any of it, and I don't want the money. Give it to the American Cancer Society, and get me out of here, Georgie."

George took his arm and guided him toward the car. Justin's legs felt like lead, and once he was in the backseat, he leaned back and closed his eyes. He'd already had more of his family—ex-family—than he wanted, and there were going to be days more of it. He was tempted to go back to Baltimore and go home. This was more than he had signed up for.

The ride was short, and Justin got out of the car when they got back to George's and went inside.

"I take it things didn't go well," Shirley said as he came into the living room.

Justin nodded his agreement. "If it's okay, I'm going to lie down." He'd had enough for a while, and some quiet would be welcome. He went to the room he was using, closed the door, and took off his shoes. When Justin lay down on the bed, it was soft and cradled him nicely. He pulled the quilt over himself and thankfully fell right to sleep. He wasn't interested in lying awake and running through what had happened, churning it over in his head again and again. All he wanted was some rest, and that was what he seemed to get.

He was back with Georgie, young and full of energy. They'd gotten their bathing suits and had ridden their bikes to one of the state parks to go swimming. After splashing and diving into the warm water, they put on their shoes and took a walk along one of the trails. They were carefree and happy, laughing, when Justin nearly tripped over a stick and thought it was a snake. He cried out, and Georgie nearly doubled over with laughter.

"Let's go back," Georgie said. "I'll race you." He took off with Justin right behind him. They reached the beach together, kicked off their shoes, and jumped into the water. In the dream, the other people in the water disappeared and it was only Georgie and him. They moved together, getting closer, exploring each other tentatively. It was new and magical.

"We should go home," Justin said, and then they were riding their bikes, pushing as the wind came up, a storm right behind them. They hurried inside to where Justin's mom and dad were waiting, looking stern. The storm broke over the house, rain pouring down as Justin stepped out with his suitcase, hesitant to step off the porch, but he had no choice. His home was disappearing from behind him.

Justin woke with a gasp, the room dark, rain lightly pelting the window. Thunder rolled in the distance. It took him a few seconds to get his bearings and remember that he was in George's guest room rather than his house in LA.

A soft knock sounded on the door, and then it cracked open. He expected Ethan, but George stuck his head in.

"Mom is making some dinner, and she said I should see if you were awake."

"I'll be out soon," Justin answered and pushed back the spread. George stepped into the room and closed the door.

"I didn't mean to push you earlier," George said as he sat on the edge of the bed.

"What happened wasn't your fault," he said, rubbing his eyes to get the sleep out of them. He wanted to lie back down and felt like he could sleep for hours, but he needed to get up or he wasn't going to sleep tonight. "It was…. I don't know. I think this whole thing with my dad finally got to me." He leaned on George's shoulder. "Sometimes I wish my life had been different."

"Everything that happens leads us to be the people we are," George said. "I wish your dad had been more reasonable and had understood that you were only explaining who you were, instead of acting like an ass." George held his hand. "I wish you hadn't had to go through all this and that you could have stayed here with me."

Justin sighed. "Me too." He turned to George. "Do you think things could have worked out? We were nineteen…."

"I don't know. But I am sure that if your dad hadn't acted the way he did, and if you hadn't left, that you'd be Justin Grove, working someplace nearby instead of Justin Hawthorne, star of the big screen and international celebrity. You made your mark on the world because of what happened."

"Yeah, but at what cost?" He sighed and tried to clear his cloudy head. "I date occasionally and spend most of my time with Ethan or my agent. Either that or I'm on set and surrounded by people all the time."

"Are you happy?" George asked.

"I love what I do, but I don't know what being happy means. Not really. Are there times when I laugh and have fun? Yes. Am I happy all the time? I doubt it. But…." Justin put an arm around George's neck. "I guess I have to say that I'm as happy as I think I can be right now." Justin smiled slightly and shrugged. "I didn't expect to be doing all this soul-searching on this trip."

"Is that good?"

Justin chuckled to relieve some of his tension. "Maybe it is. I obviously have some issues that I'm still trying to work through. And a lot of them revolve around my father. I guess they were lurking somewhere in the back of my head waiting to come out." He blinked a few times. "I had the strangest dream. It was about you and how we used to go swimming at the park. But then everything got messed up."

"Dreams are like that. Our minds weave everything together." George stood and went to the window to push the curtains open. "This has been a weird spring. One day it's summery, and the next, winter looks like it's going to try to make an appearance." George turned back around. "We should get ready for dinner. Mom will have it about ready."

"A home-cooked meal," Justin said as his stomach rumbled. He'd eaten in restaurants and at commissaries or had things brought to his trailer for years. The kitchen at his house was rarely used unless Ethan decided he wanted to make something. Justin certainly never had time.

Justin pushed himself to his feet, and when George came closer, Justin hugged him tight, closing his eyes. George felt the same, or largely the same, in his arms as Justin remembered. George was thicker, more grown up, stronger, but he fit the way he always had. "I missed you," he said softly. In his movies, Justin could call upon an emotional response easily. It came naturally to him. His real emotions he kept buried down deep, but they surfaced now in the quiet, with Georgie. "I thought about you a lot. When I first got to Los Angeles, I used to turn so I could share what I was seeing with you, but you weren't there."

"You got on well enough," George said and held him a little tighter. "Fuck, I missed you too. When you were just gone, I thought someone had taken you or something. I went over to your house. Your dad was at work, and your mother was worried."

"I had to get away," Justin said, his voice breaking. He clamped his eyes closed.

"Ethan thinks that something happened to you that day, and that's why you never came back," George said, and Justin nodded but kept quiet. "Have you told anyone?"

"No. And I won't. So don't ever ask about it." Justin swallowed. He'd pushed that from his mind and refused to think about it. Hell, he'd clouded what had happened with other things and done his best to obscure and change it. He purposely hadn't thought about it in years. Justin pulled away. "Please don't bring it up again."

"Okay," George agreed in a soft voice. "I'm sorry."

George held his gaze, and Justin knew he should turn away, but the heat held him in its spell. He had men and women look at him lustfully all the time. He usually ignored it. Who cared about the lustful fantasies of strangers? But this was Georgie, and he was mesmerized.

Justin flinched slightly when George touched his cheek, running his fingers along his jawline. "Georgie, I…."

"I missed your eyes and the way you looked at me," George said, cutting him off. "No one ever has that same way again. Do you remember our first kiss? We were in this room, supposedly studying math, but it was anatomy that got a workout." Georgie smiled, and his eyes darkened, tongue wetting his lips.

"I remember." Justin wet his own lips as George moved closer.

"I never stopped thinking about you. I used to wonder if you were all right and if you found someone else."

"Nope. There was no one to replace you." Maybe that was why he'd found it relatively easy to stay single and unattached. He'd always said it was because he was so busy, but the truth was that he didn't have any real interest, because no one else was George. He put his hands on George's shoulders and leaned in closer, determined to answer the question of whether things would be the same.

A sharp knock on the door made Justin step back. He took a deep breath to calm his heart and opened the door.

"Dinner is in a few minutes," Shirley said.

"Thank you. We'll be right there." Justin left the door open and grabbed his shoes off the floor. The moment had passed, and he'd clearly been about to make a stupid mistake. Getting involved with George was a disaster in the making. Justin was only going to be here a few days, and he wasn't about to give George false hope—or himself, for that matter. His life was in California now, and he had many people depending on him.

George looked strange, and he kept his gaze anywhere in the room but on Justin.

"We should go," Justin said.

"Yeah," George said. "Dinner is almost ready."

Justin's hand tingled, and as George took a step toward the door, he realized that if he let it go this time, there wouldn't be another. He'd have rejected George, and in the short time they had left, he wasn't likely to be given another chance. All the arguments about why he should stay away raced through his head, and Justin dismissed them all. He took George by the arm, turned him around, and pushed him against the wall next to the door.

Damn, George was gorgeous, his eyes like deep pools. Justin cupped his chin lightly, the stubble rough against his hands. God, he liked that feeling. George was all man, and he liked that he could feel it, smell it, and damned if it didn't draw him in like a moth to flame. He leaned closer, and George parted his lips. Justin didn't hesitate this time.

He touched his lips to George's and then deepened the kiss. Energy, pure and hot, shot up his back—this was what he'd been missing all these years. George wrapped his arms around Justin's shoulders, pulling him closer. Desire, raw and white-hot, shot through Justin, and he pressed a knee between George's so he could get him hip to hip.

His entire body thrummed with the same excitement as a movie premiere. He was electric and on fire. George tasted rich and slightly spicy, almost exactly the way he remembered. George was less tentative, cupping the back of Justin's head and giving as good as he got. Justin's lips tingled from the pressure and excitement. He had to breathe, but he didn't want to back away for a second. This was what he'd waited on for seven years. He'd acted out being in love and portrayed broken hearts on-screen, but never had he imagined the power and headiness that George gave him.

"Oh God," George breathed when he pulled away. Justin inhaled and pounced once again, needing to taste and feel George. He pressed him back against the wall, hard, George's jeans-encased cock pressing to Justin's hip. He reached around, sliding his hands along George's hips, cupping his butt and pressing harder. He'd climb into him if he could. All these years of wanting, and there was no way he could possibly get enough in just a few seconds.

"Yeah," Justin said when they surfaced for air. He gasped and struggled not to make too much noise. This was George's house and all, but he didn't want questions from Ethan about what was happening, because he didn't know himself.

"I need a few seconds," George whispered and left the room, going right across the hall to the bathroom. Justin stood still, willing some of the heat from his face to abate. He sat on the edge of the bed and put on his shoes. When George came out of the bathroom, Justin followed him down the hall to the kitchen.

Shirley and Ethan were putting dishes on the table. "Did you have a good sleep?" Shirley asked without turning around. Ethan set the bowl of salad on the table. He caught Justin's eye for a second and then helped Shirley bring over the rest of their dinner before leaving the room.

"Yes, I did. I think after all the travel I needed a few hours' sleep." Justin yawned. He was finally feeling rested. "Can I help?"

"It's almost ready," Shirley said.

"I put the box of things from the house in your room," Ethan said when he returned. "They're near your suitcase."

"Thanks, Ethan," Justin said and pulled out the chair that George indicated. "It smells awesome."

Shirley brought over a gorgeous roast beef, and his stomach lurched.

"I remember a certain young man at this table who used to ask to go to church with us because when we got home, I'd have made his favorite meal." She set the platter on the table.

"You made this for me?" He reached out to Shirley and took her hand, lightly squeezing her fingers.

"Of course I did, and I whipped up some of my horseradish sauce as well. You used to eat that like it was going out of style." She sat down and folded her hands. Without thinking, Justin fell into the old routine, and Shirley said a soft prayer of thanks for the food, adding a thank-you for the guests around her table at the end. Justin hadn't said a prayer at a meal since the last one he'd shared with George and his family years before. His family was never the "pray together" type. They'd been more the "grab and go sit in front of the television" type of family.

"Thank you. You're going to spoil me," Justin told her.

"She showed me her secrets," Ethan said, though Justin doubted those secrets would actually be put into action. Still, he smiled to send Ethan a vote of confidence while Shirley stood to cut the roast. She put a slice on a plate and handed it to George, who filled the rest of the plate and passed it around. When Justin's plate was set in front of him, his mouth watered and he reached for the horseradish sauce.

Justin cut and tasted a piece, and he was in heaven. Once everyone was served, they sat and ate.

"Do you have plans for tomorrow?" Shirley asked, and Justin turned to George. He hadn't made any, and he didn't think there were any appointments until the minister dropped by on Tuesday.

"Maybe we can go into town and look around," George suggested. "We were at the diner today, but that's all."

Justin wasn't in any huge hurry to do anything in particular and was willing to ride along with George wherever he wanted to go. "I have to have some time to read through the script, but that will only take a few hours. I can do that after dinner and in the morning." Justin was determined never to let others tell him what work he should take. If he liked the script, he'd do it. If not, he'd commit one of the sins of

Hollywood and walk away from twenty million. He wasn't going to do a bad movie just for the money.

"Do all actors read their scripts like you do?"

"I'd like to think so. But a lot of them contract for the film and then try to fight for a better script. I'd rather know if it's a quality film up front. So many actors are riding high, and they think that they can carry any film. Then you have that *Twilight* actor who went off on his own, did a bad film, and now no one cares about him anymore. He thought he was the gift to moviegoers everywhere and could carry the film alone." Justin snickered. "It might have done better if he'd spent half the film with his clothes falling off or something."

George laughed because he knew exactly what Justin was talking about—biggest movie disappointment ever.

"I don't want that to happen, so I read my scripts, make notes, and go over them with my agent. Then I let him fight the battles for me. And Roy is very good at that. He really likes this script, and that says something, but I have to like it because I'm the one who's going to spend months on sets, in sound booths, and everywhere else to make sure it's perfect."

"Didn't you just finish shooting?" George asked.

"Yeah. I'll be working on this one and then have to spend some time working with the director and editor to correct mistakes or even do minor reshoots. All while I'm making the next film. It can be a very grueling life."

"Do you have to do that many films like that?"

"No. But I'm still new, and I want to build up a body of work so that I can take it easy later if I decide to. No one questions Tom Hanks's screen credentials, and I want to be like him. Make quality films and get meaty roles that everyone remembers." Justin took a bite and turned toward the front window, groaning at the milling crowd. Ethan sighed and stood. "I'll take care of it." He went to the front window and pulled the curtains.

"What's going on?" Shirley asked.

"Press," Ethan said. "Let me deal with it." He left the house, and Justin went back to eating while the others got up.

"Please don't. We deal with this all the time. The more attention they get, the more they hound. Ethan is explaining why I'm here, and if they have any decency, they'll leave. The ones in Hollywood would stick around, but I'm willing to bet the ones here will be less aggressive."

Justin continued eating while the others remained seated, looking nervous. Finally, Ethan came in from outside, grinning.

"They're leaving. I gave a brief statement to one of the reporters that you're here to attend your father's funeral, and I asked that you be given the same respect and care that they would want in a similar situation. That seemed to get to them, and they packed up and are leaving."

"Thanks, Ethan. But we're going to have to be careful for the next few days. Your statement, while helpful, has just confirmed that I'm in town, and that confirmation is going to run on every station for days." Justin was disappointed, but he didn't see any alternative. "I may need to leave if people decide they're going to camp out in front of the house in order to get a glimpse of me." He turned to Shirley and George. "I don't want to disrupt your lives."

"Oh, honey. A little excitement around here will do me good." She patted his hand. "So don't you worry about us. We're glad to have both of you with us." She picked up her fork and then set it down again. "Do you want some more?"

"Yes, please," he said with a grin. It had been a long time since he'd had someone other than Ethan behind him full force, and judging by the set of George's jaw, he had three people now.

"We're all here for you," George said.

"I appreciate that, but I shouldn't need it, and you shouldn't be put into this situation." Justin had chosen this life, and he knew there were costs, but all the people around him shouldn't have to pay the price for his fame. Ethan had chosen to stick by him and be his friend, companion, and personal assistant. But he felt like he was stifling Ethan's life as well. It was like his life and career were so big they were consuming him and enveloping the people in his life.

"Sweetheart. You're here for a few days. George and I can certainly take care of ourselves for that long. You just relax and don't worry about it," Shirley said.

Justin nearly jumped out of his seat when George gently patted his leg. The gesture was supposed to be reassuring, at least he thought so, but even once his hand was gone, Justin could still feel it. And that was bad—he wanted George like a starving man craved bread. He knew it was a bad idea to get involved with him. It would give them both false hope.

Justin tried to figure out how he was going to get George out of his mind. He started by finishing his dinner and taking his dishes to the sink. Then he excused himself after thanking Shirley for a memorable meal and hurried to his room. He needed something to take his mind off the issue at hand, so he grabbed his tablet and pulled up the script he was supposed to read.

It didn't work very well. He lay on the bed, trying to get into the script in front of him, but his attention kept wandering to the voices that drifted down the hall. Dishes clinked and laughter occasionally drifted in. But what got him every time was when the deep richness of George's voice reached his ears. It pulled him out of his reading every single time. He had to get this done, so he concentrated harder. It got easier when the house quieted.

The script was good and dynamic, the dialogue not stilted or dumb-sounding. Sometimes these things read as though they were written by high school students. Now, there was nothing wrong with playing high-school-aged characters, but when a script read as though it had been written by them, Justin had a problem. Eventually he was able to really get into the story and let it take over. Before he knew it, he'd reached the end of it and smiled. He pulled out his phone and called Roy.

"Well, what did you think?" Roy asked.

"I liked the script, so agree to the contract, and I'll sign it next week."

"The producers really want to get you locked in as soon as possible," Roy said.

"Tell them you have my verbal commitment and that I never go back on my word. I'll sign the contract in your office next week, and this is a done deal as long as there isn't anything in the fine print that will be detrimental."

"You did get that you'll have a leading lady and that there are a couple love scenes?" Roy pointed out.

"That's no big deal." He'd done those before, and he'd do them again.

"I didn't want you to be uncomfortable," Roy explained.

"What the hell? Did you take some sensitivity training class while I've been gone?" Justin joked. "Knock it off and be the real Roy. He's a pain in my ass, but I understand him."

"I was trying to be nice because of what you're going through."

He could almost see Roy rolling his eyes. The man could be overly dramatic to say the least.

"That's the Roy I know and hate," Justin jabbed.

"Ha-ha," Roy countered.

"Seriously, go through that contract with a fine-tooth comb. I'm not going to have some stupid behavior or drug-testing clause in it like they did with *Stars*. Remember?"

"A lot of producers are requiring it as a matter of course."

Justin smiled. "You tell them that when they submit to the testing and have the director do it as well, then I will. I have never warranted it, and I never will." That shit was poison. "If they ask why, tell them that if they're so interested in pee in cups, I'll make sure to have more than enough delivered to them."

Roy laughed. "I'll see what I can do."

"Thanks, Roy. Call me if you have any questions."

"When is the funeral?"

Justin sighed. "Tuesday we meet with the minister, and Wednesday is the service. My dad made all the arrangements, but I suspect we'll stop in tomorrow to see to any details. Mostly I'm taking this as quiet time."

"Good. As much as I hate having you there, I'm glad you're getting some rest. The next six months are going to be very busy."

"I know, Roy. My schedule is off the charts." They said their good-byes, and Roy promised to review the contract closely. He hung up, and Justin closed his eyes. So damn much had happened today, and he was trying to get his head around it all.

HE JOINED the others in the living room as they were watching some cable show. Justin sat next to George and soaked in some of his warmth. Even in the house, the colder nights seemed to seep into him.

"Did Roy get what he needed?" George asked.

"Yeah. He's happy, and I'm pooped," Justin said. He had thought he'd be up late because of the change in the time zones. He hadn't realized how late it was until he saw the time on the television and it was after midnight. "Is that right?"

"Yes," Shirley said. "You youngsters can stay up as late as you want. But I'm about to turn into a pumpkin."

She said good night to each of them and went off to bed. Justin closed his eyes, content to relax where he was, but it became apparent that his long days were catching up with him. He stood and went down the hall to bed as well.

Justin used the bathroom and changed into a T-shirt and shorts. Then he returned to the bedroom and closed the door most of the way. He liked to have fresh air when he slept. He got into bed and lay with his head on the soft pillow, listening as the house quieted.

His door slid open a little, and Justin tensed.

"Do you need anything?" Ethan asked.

"No, I'm fine. Good night," Justin said as Ethan put the door back the way it had been. Justin rolled over, chastising himself. He'd hoped that the door opening meant George was coming in to see him. His mind and body both thrummed with energy just from the hope.

The hallway lights went out, and Justin followed the last footsteps down the hall with his hearing. He knew it was George, and he heard the footsteps stop outside his door. He rolled over to face it, ready to welcome George in with him. But the footsteps continued on, and then the door down the hall opened and closed. Justin sighed, closed his eyes, and tried to sleep.

CHAPTER 4

GEORGE GOT up late. He hadn't slept for much of the night. His body and mind were well aware that Justin was in the next room. He'd actually stopped outside Justin's room before going to bed, debating whether he should step inside. Every fiber of his body had urged him to do it. But he'd never been one to think with his dick, and he didn't follow where it had pointed. Instead he'd gone with his head and fear and walked past the door to his own room—then spent much of the night with a hard-on, second-guessing that decision.

Granted, he wasn't sure if Justin would have welcomed his advance. He'd even had a cover story that he was just checking to make sure Justin was comfortable. But that kiss before dinner—there was no way he could get it out of his mind. Just thinking about it sent heat racing through him, and he wanted a repeat. Hell, he wanted to strip Justin naked and see if he looked the same as he had before he left. He wanted to know what Justin felt like, skin to skin. It had been seven years of remembering and longing. He'd missed his friend so much. Hell, George wasn't going to admit it to anyone, but he'd never stopped loving Justin. That was why his few attempted relationships had failed miserably. None of them were Justin, and they hadn't measured up to the memories.

Mostly he spent the night berating himself for not having the courage to find out if he could actually have what he wanted most.

George padded out of his room in the late morning, bleary-eyed and half-awake. His brain was only partially functioning, but he got a major wake-up call when the bathroom door opened and Justin stepped out in just a pair of hip-hugging dark blue shorts. George's mouth went dry, and he swallowed.

The images he'd seen in Justin's movies paled by comparison to the real man standing in front of him. Justin was toned and tanned but not bulky. He was the marathon runner, the man who was in it for the long haul, with sleek, defined muscles that George longed to reach out and touch. He'd definitely changed from the young man George had known into a stunning example of male eroticism. No wonder people wanted to take pictures of this man. Hell, if he thought he could get away with it, George would run back into his room to get his phone so he could snap some himself. Those pictures would fuel his fantasies for years.

"I'm sorry. Did you need the bathroom?" Justin asked.

George made some sort of sound, but even he had no idea what it meant, other than maybe a simple "Fuck me now." He blinked a few times to try to clear his head and opened his mouth again. But only gibberish came out. A third try yielded better results. "Holy crap." George wanted to slap his hands over his mouth.

Justin looked down and then back to him. "What's gotten into you?" Justin asked, and George glanced around and grabbed Justin by the hand. He yanked him into his bedroom, closed the door, and placed his hands against the heat of Justin's chest.

"You expect me to talk when you're standing around like this?" George asked, his mouth dry once again. "God, you were always handsome, but not like this."

"I have to look good on-screen, and the camera always adds weight, so…."

"Screw the camera. Holy crap." George slowly let his hands glide over Justin's smooth skin. It took him a second to realize he was petting Justin, up and down. His ability to think had obviously snapped some time ago. Justin leaned in, capturing his lips, and George gave himself over completely to the sensation.

His head pounded and his heart raced as Justin pulled him close. He wound his arms around Justin, placing his hands flat against his powerful back. Justin deepened the kiss, sending more and more passion running through him. George held on tight as Justin propelled him back until he fell onto the soft sheets of his bed. "What do you want?"

"You have to ask?" George retorted breathlessly.

"Yes."

Justin sucked on his ear, and George moaned softly, quivering with increased excitement.

"I know what I want."

Justin tugged at his T-shirt, and George pulled his hands away from his own explorations. Stitches tore as Justin nearly ripped the shirt from him.

"It's been seven years since I touched you. Seven long years since I've been able to hold and kiss you." Justin was already working at George's pants. "Seven fucking years."

He seemed to be having trouble getting the fastener undone, and George helped him so he didn't end up with shredded jeans. Justin stepped back, breathing hard, staring at him with eyes as deep as the night.

"Justin, is this a good idea?"

Justin growled and leaned over him. "Fucking hell no. It's a terrible idea."

Justin yanked at the bottom of his pant legs, and they slid down and off, leaving him in a small pair of dark blue briefs that George figured were going to be ripped off him, judging by the feral look in Justin's eyes.

"I want you so damn much that I'm willing to risk it. Are you?"

George nodded and croaked out a yes.

Justin pulled off George's underwear and pushed his own shorts to the floor. Justin's cock, thick, long, and full, jutted straight and proud from his groin. "This isn't going to be pretty or last very long," Justin growled half under his breath as he crawled up onto the bed.

Justin claimed his lips hard and with a force that took George's breath away.

"I hope you have lube and condoms."

George glanced at the bedside table and then back to Justin, who kissed him once again and then slid down his body. Justin gave him no warning before he opened his gorgeous lips and slid them down his cock. What little breath George had been able to catch flew from him, and he panted while Justin sucked him to within an inch of his sanity.

"Jus," George cried as the old nickname came from somewhere deep inside. Justin had hated any nicknames growing up, and George had been the only one to get away with one. He pushed his hips forward, enthralled by the way his cock disappeared into Justin's mouth.

Justin pulled back, George's cock slapping against his belly. "I've waited too damn long to have you again."

"I'm here right now," George groaned as Justin gripped his cock, sucking him into his mouth ever so slowly, his lips tight around it. God in heaven, George had dreamed of those lips and of Justin touching him. He'd dreamed of being the object of Justin's intense gaze ever since their last time together. No one could touch him the way Justin did. George knew that, but he also knew that their time together was going to be short and…. Those thoughts flew from his head as Justin sucked him deep and pressed two fingers in his mouth alongside George's cock.

George stilled and waited, placing his feet on the side rail of the bed. Justin withdrew his fingers, using his tongue to tease the underside of his cock, and then pressed those fingers to George's opening, slowly breaching him. George threw his head back and swallowed the loud, throaty moan that threatened to erupt from him. Justin knew how to play his body. He seemed to remember all the things that would drive him wild. What struck him most was that Justin remembered. George had as well. He'd played Justin's body over and over in his mind so many times.

He quivered under Justin and let his arms fall over his head, stretching and letting Justin take over… for now.

"I'm warning you, I can't…." George moaned softly, thankful again that the door was closed. Justin kept sucking, harder, driving him toward release. George had been hoping for more than a blowjob the first time with Justin, if there could be another time for them on this visit. But he'd take whatever he could get. He hadn't expected to ever see Justin again, and being alone with him and intimate was more than he'd ever dreamed.

George pulled away, breathing hard to try to keep oxygen flowing to his head. "Not like this," he gasped and pulled Justin up far enough that he could kiss him.

"Georgie…."

"I have no illusions about what's going to happen," he said when they broke their sloppy, wet kiss. "But I want you, Justin, for as long as you're here." He patted his chest. "Do you hear me? I'll take whatever time I have with you for as long as I can." He pulled him forward and fumbled to get the drawer open on the nightstand. Justin seemed to understand because he stopped kissing long enough to find a condom and some lube.

When Justin straightened up, George scooted back on the bed to get his head on the pillow. He watched with rapt attention as Justin tossed the lube and condoms on the bed. He pulled more out of the drawer and tossed those there too.

"Justin, how many are you going to need?" George asked.

Justin jammed the door closed, turning his now-black-as-night eyes on him. "That might do for now."

His voice was husky as hell, and that sent another wave of desire running through George. God, Justin was a stud, as hot as they came. George quivered when he joined him on the bed again. He expected Justin to go for the lube and condoms, but he ignored them, stroking up his chest and then leaning forward to kiss and lick a trail behind his wandering hands.

"If we're going to do this, then we'll do it right."

He slowly raised his leg and straddled him, cock pointing toward the ceiling, and fuck, what a cock it was. Long and thick. If Justin ever wanted to change the kind of movies he did, George figured he was more than qualified.

Slowly, Justin massaged his chest, tweaking his nipples while moving upward, that glorious cock getting closer and closer to his lips. George parted his lips and raised his head, stretching his lips around it.

Justin's flavor burst on his tongue, salty and bittersweet, and he loved it. Cradling Justin's balls in his hand, he sucked him harder and closer, taking as much of him as he could. This was a fantasy come true.

"Jesus, Georgie," Justin breathed, loudly sucking air into his lungs.

He didn't try to talk but hummed his happiness and continued sucking. Justin rocked slowly, rolling his hips, and damn, he wished he could watch that too. He wanted it all at once, but that wasn't possible.

Justin slid back, his butt over George's hips, looking at him like a wild cat. "I used to wonder if I'd ever get you like this again." Justin reached behind his body, and George groaned, wondering what Justin had in mind. He found out when Justin wrapped his fingers firmly around George's cock. "You always responded to me like no one else ever has."

A million questions flew through his head, but now wasn't the time for any of them. "I want you, Jus."

"I know, Georgie. I want you too."

He knelt on the bed and reached for the lube and then fished around in the pile of condoms. He ripped one open and rolled it on. George watched his fingers as they worked. He reached to stroke him, but Justin distracted him with fingers of his own. He grabbed the slick and prepared him.

George saw stars; that was the only way to describe it. "I wish...."

"I know," Justin agreed as their eyes met, and words weren't necessary.

They both wished things were different. Justin leaned forward, enthralling George as he pressed to his opening and held there. George's chest heaved with anticipation, and he pulled Justin into a kiss, meeting him halfway.

He bit Justin's lip as he entered him. George hadn't meant to, but the sensation was so intense. He soothed the skin with his tongue and was relieved to taste no blood.

"Liked that, did you?"

"Fuck yes, but you're damn big. You know that." He arched his back, and Justin stilled, letting him adjust to the welcome intrusion. When he pressed forward, George sighed and groaned again when he felt Justin's hips against his ass.

"You...." Justin kissed him hard. "You make me want things I know I can't have." Justin scooped him into his arms and held him closer.

"I know," George said and clutched at Justin as he rolled those amazing hips and drove him to oblivion. George could only hold on. He'd dreamed of this and wanted it to last. But Justin seemed frantic now, and George's entire being seemed in tune with that, like Justin's franticness was contagious. He moved with him, rocking his hips in time with Justin's. He reached between them to stroke his cock, and Justin batted his hand away, one of his taking its place.

That was heaven, knowing his own body and pleasure were out of his hands, literally, and in Justin's control. He gritted his teeth and slid a hand around Justin's neck. He needed a way to steady himself.

"I have you, Georgie," Justin said. "I won't let you fall or be carried away."

He knew Justin was referring metaphorically to the height of sex and passion, but part of him wanted to believe that would extend to things outside the bedroom. But he didn't dare hope, not really. He threw his head back and let the intensity wash over him.

Justin was amazing, fantastic, and un-fucking-believable. He didn't seem to pay any attention to his own needs but stoked George's with each and every movement. George could hardly see, his eyes were so filled with moisture. The room swam, and George held on, wanting more, needing all that Justin had to give, and when it was too much and Justin had driven him to the edge of his control, George plummeted over the edge, grasping at the bedding to anchor himself and keep from flying to pieces.

George lay still, listening to Justin pant above him. He wondered how long it would take before Justin realized what they'd done and put distance between them. George expected it and gasped softly when Justin slowly disengaged their bodies and then pulled him closer, holding him tightly to his chest.

The room was steamy, moisture from their bodies clinging to nearly everything. George didn't dare move or say anything for fear that the spell between them, which seemed as thin as a hair, would break and Justin would leave and he'd be left with nothing. That was the most likely result of things at the end of the week, but he didn't want that to happen too soon.

"I think we're going to need to get up and make an appearance or else your mother and Ethan are going to know exactly what we've been doing."

George snuggled closer. "Do you think they haven't figured it out?" He turned to the clock by the side of the bed. "It's after eleven, and I rarely sleep this late."

Justin released him and sat back, taking care of the condom and dropping it in the waste can. "How about we forget about them for a little while longer, then?" Justin chuckled and pounced on him when George began to get up. Justin fell back on the bed and ran his fingers up his side.

George giggled like a kid and squirmed away. "You always tickled."

"And you always made the most amazing laugh when I did. Just like now, it's so bright, like there's not a care in it."

George settled when Justin stopped tickling. "That's the illusion, isn't it? You can tickle me and I laugh, but it doesn't mean that I'm happy. It only means that I have an involuntary response." He sat back and looked Justin up and down. "That was our problem, I think. We thought we were happy together. At least I did."

"We were," Justin said.

"No. We were naïve, but I don't think we were happy. Because if we had been, you wouldn't have left."

Justin lay down next to him, staring up at the ceiling. "You don't understand. There were…."

George rolled onto his side. "You don't get to run away from me again, like some thief in the night." He did his best to keep the heat and hurt out of his voice.

"I didn't. I had to go. I know I hurt you, and I'm sorry for that, but it was something I had to do, and you need to trust me on that." Justin turned away. "This was a mistake."

George grabbed Justin's shoulder to stop him from getting up. "This was not a mistake. This, what we had just now, felt right. Don't mix up the heat between us with what you did seven years ago. They are two different things, whether you want to think so or not." He scooted closer. "You can't tell me you didn't feel the pull, the need...."

"I did, but it's.... Nothing has changed. I left and the years have passed. Now we're together again, but I'm going to have to leave."

George smacked Justin on the shoulder, and he rubbed it. "This bloody time you damn well better say good-bye and not leave me wondering what I've done to push you away."

"Is that what you thought? That you did something wrong?" Justin whirled around.

"Well, there has to be an explanation, and that's the most likely one. I wasn't good enough for you or didn't make you happy, so you had to leave. Instead of facing me, you took the coward's way out. And you're trying to do it again."

"You did nothing wrong, and it broke my heart to leave, but I didn't have a choice. You have to believe me and take it on faith. That's all I can tell you."

Justin's eyes pleaded with him more vigorously than his voice. He leaned closer, his lips so close George could feel his breath.

"But I will say once again, cross my heart and pinky swear, that I never left because of anything you did or because I didn't love you."

Justin got up off the bed and pulled on his shorts. He left the room before George could figure out what was happening, and he stared at the closed door with his mouth open. What the hell had just happened?

A few minutes later, Justin burst back into the room, kicking the door closed behind him. He grabbed George's hand and placed something in it. George brought his hand closer and opened it.

"Do you remember? You gave me that when we graduated from high school. After the party my parents threw, we got in their car, and they thought we were going to another party when all we did was head out to park."

"Yeah, I do. I saved for a month from my job so I could get you the chain. Mom was going to Harrisburg, and I asked to go along but didn't tell her what I wanted, and when she went to the department store at the mall, I snuck away to one of the jewelry stores and got it for you. She wondered where I went, and I said I was at the Orange Julius getting something to drink. She would have been mad at the money I spent, but I wanted you to have it."

"As you can see, I kept it. I pawned most everything I had when I left. I took all the things that were mine that had any value. That and my savings, and I got across the country. I never pawned this. I would have starved before I did that, because if this was gone, then so was the last of you that I had." Justin's hand shook.

"I believe you." George handed the chain back to Justin. "And I can't believe you kept that all this time."

"Of course I did," Justin said and leaned in, kissing him ever so gently. "I didn't hear your mother or Ethan in the house, so I think we need to get cleaned up and figure out what those two are up to."

"I think we better," George agreed. He jumped off the bed and peered out the door. Justin was right—the house was quiet. He hurried into the bathroom, where he showered, and then raced back to his room in only a towel to change.

Once he was presentable, he wandered out. Justin's door was open and the room empty. He still didn't hear anyone in the house. In the kitchen he found the coffeepot on and poured a mug before checking out back. The sun had come out, and his mother and Ethan were out there.

"Justin," he called.

"Living room."

"You know my mother has Ethan working in the garden?" He pulled open the sliding door and stepped outside.

"You're up," Ethan said and turned away. George could have sworn he heard him snicker.

"I was wondering if you were going to get up sometime today," his mother added. "Ethan and I had breakfast hours ago. He's been helping me get some of my beds cleaned up. I'll make you some lunch soon."

Justin joined George, and they both wandered out into the yard. Spring was just beginning to take hold. The grass was greening up, and some of the perennials were sprouting. In small patches around the yard, crocuses were blooming and other bulbs were getting ready to open.

"Did you check your e-mail this morning?" Justin asked Ethan.

"Yeah. There was a contract that I sent to your tablet for you to look at. Other than that, there were just the usual things that I answered. There are multiple fan e-mails that were received. I forwarded them to the publicists for them to handle. There was one that caught my eye, and I sent that to the tablet as well. You might want to see if you'd like to answer that one yourself, and we can handle it from there."

Justin sipped from his mug and sat in one of the lawn chairs. "I forgot how nice spring can be here."

"Wait until tomorrow—it will be cold again I'm sure," George said, and his mother shushed him. He sat in the other chair while his mother and Ethan finished up what they were doing.

LUNCH WAS nice, if a little strange, with George's mother and Ethan sharing looks and he and Justin doing the same, mainly out of curiosity as to what was up with those two and because George couldn't figure out a way not to glance at Justin. He drew his interest, and there was no other way to describe it.

"Will you go to the hardware store for me this afternoon? I need some garden edging, and my hose didn't make it through the winter," his mother said.

"I drained it last fall," George said.

"It was old, and the cold did it in," she said and took a bite of her sandwich.

It was a simple lunch, sandwiches made from the leftover roast beef, and his mother's special potato salad, with hot tea to ward off the chill around the edges.

"I'll go right after lunch," George agreed and glanced at Ethan and Justin to see if either of them wanted to ride along. Neither seemed interested, and that was fine. It was a short errand. When he had finished eating, George took care of his dishes and got his keys and wallet.

"I'll ride along," Justin said, and Ethan shared a smirk with Shirley.

George knew they were aware of what he and Justin had done that morning and had probably discussed it while they were working in the yard. He wasn't sure how he felt about that, but he was grateful they weren't talking about it outright. At least it didn't seem like he was going to be spending the next week blushing every five minutes.

"Give me a few minutes," Justin added, and he left the table after thanking George's mother for the wonderful lunch.

George was a little surprised when Justin kissed her cheek and then strode down the hall. He returned with a hat and sunglasses as well as a hoodie sweatshirt, which he shrugged into and zipped up.

"You really think that's going to keep you from being noticed?" George teased.

"Lots of kids wear hoodies, and they are a good way to hide your face from a casual observer. At least in LA, no one seems to notice you if you're dressed like this."

"It seems hokey," George said, heading for the door.

"It's what I have," Justin said from behind him. "I could put on a face mask and walk through town as the Wicked Witch of the West. I do have a few contacts in Hollywood. But I think that's going to defeat the purpose of not garnering too much attention."

"Smartass," George quipped and opened his car door.

"Let's go. It's a Monday afternoon, and most people will be at work or in school, so it should be fairly quiet."

George buckled in and waited for Justin before backing down the drive. "How do you want to handle it if someone does recognize you?"

"As long as they're respectful, I'll be nice and talk to them. Sometimes people are pushy, and if that happens, I'll go right back to the car and lock the doors." That was Justin-speak for "We'll have to get the hell out of there."

"Okay." George reached across the console and took Justin's hand. "I'm sure it will be fine."

"So am I or I'd stay home and out of sight." Justin closed his fingers around George's. "Your mother and Ethan know what happened this morning."

"Yeah, they do. Those looks were pretty meaningful. I suspect my mother is going to want to talk to me about it at some point."

"What are you going to tell her?"

George slowed for an intersection. "That we have our eyes open and that we aren't eighteen any longer." He was doing his best to think about the here and now instead of what was to come. His phone rang, and George pulled into a parking spot before answering it, leaving the motor running. "Hello?"

"This is Marcia at Hoover's Funeral Home. We have a few questions. It's our understanding that Mr. Grove's funeral will be held here in our chapel."

"Yes."

"When he preplanned, there were no hymns specified."

"Okay. Hold on," George said and explained to Justin what the call was about. "Do you have any that you'd like?"

Justin was instantly thoughtful. "'Bringing in the Sheaves.' I always liked that one, and my mother's favorite was 'Amazing Grace.'" Justin wiped his eyes. "She always liked 'Onward Christian Soldiers' as well." George relayed the message and realized that maybe as much as Justin was putting on a show of strength, this funeral was turning into more than he'd expected. Yes, they were burying his father, but to Justin, he was burying both his parents.

"Good. We need one more," Marcia said.

"Just pick one that's commonly used and easy for people to sing. That should work very well."

"All right, I'll do that. Thank you." She ended the call, and George put his phone in his pocket and turned off the engine.

"It's okay to be upset," George told Justin. "I know you're holding on to the resentment and pain."

"What else am I supposed to do?"

"Let it go. It's in the past, and that experience went into making you the person and the success you are today. Holding on to the pain isn't helping you. I know he didn't disown me, but he drove you away, and I was able to forgive him for what he did to me and to us."

"But he wasn't your father," Justin said.

"No, he wasn't." George opened his door. "But he did help bring about a heartache that cut me deeply for a long time. When I decided to let it go, I started to heal and get past it." He got out of the car and waited while Justin put on his glasses and raised his hood before getting out of the car. "I'm only saying it's something to think about."

"I don't know if I can," Justin said softly.

"It isn't as though it's something that happens overnight. But it means that you can get on with your life without this millstone around your neck." He got out and closed his door, waiting for Justin. They went into the hardware store, and George waved to Mr. Lowell behind the counter and continued into the store.

"Shirley said she needed a hose and edging."

"Over here," George directed and grabbed a thick reel of hose. Justin took it, and George found the edging his mother liked. He got three packages and then wandered through the store to see if there was anything else he needed.

"Hey, Mark," George said as he passed a guy he'd gone to school with.

Mark nodded gruffly, his lip curled slightly. He grunted a hello and continued down the aisle. He and Mark had never been friends, and they certainly never would be, but that surly a greeting was unusual. George turned to ask Justin to get another reel of hose, figuring they might as well have some extra, but Justin was gone.

George went back the way he'd come, but there was no sign of Justin. The store wasn't that big, and he couldn't get lost. He retraced their steps to the front and found the hose on the front counter. "Your friend said he'd wait for you outside," Mr. Lowell explained.

"Okay," George said, wondering what had happened.

Mark approached the desk and asked about pipe fittings. Mr. Lowell went to help him, and George figured he might as well finish looking before finding Justin.

It took another fifteen minutes, and he ended up with a couple of sprinklers and a watering wand for the hose before he was done. "How is it going, sir?" he asked when he went back up to the register.

"Slow," Mr. Lowell answered. He was never a man of long explanations or a particularly sunny disposition. "The good weather helps."

"I think it helps everyone."

"Not snowblower salesmen," Mr. Lowell cracked.

"Okay, I'll give you that," George agreed. He paid for his purchases and hauled them out of the store. He peered into the car, but he didn't see Justin. After stashing everything in the car, he wandered up and down the street, peering into shop windows. He finally found Justin in the used clothing store a few doors down from the hardware store.

"There you are," George said as he approached Justin, who jumped a little and then went back to fanning his way through a rack of men's shirts without actually looking at any of them. George followed his gaze to the front window.

"I wanted to take a look at the town," he said lamely, still watching out front.

"We can go whenever you're ready," George said, and Justin nodded but kept watching. George wondered what was going on, but he figured he'd check for anything interesting while they were there. He looked through a rack of pants.

"I'm ready when you are," Justin said, and George gave up trying to figure out what was up. As they left the store, Justin scanned the street, sliding his sunglasses back on, and George did the same, trying to figure out what he was looking for. There was no activity other than a truck in the middle of the block that pulled out as he watched. George led the way back to the car as the truck sped by. The horn blared as it passed, and George turned.

"Some people are idiots," he muttered under his breath and opened the car door. Justin was quiet the entire ride back to the house. He kept turning to look behind them and stared at the mirror on his side of the car. "What happened?"

"Nothing. I might have been recognized and wanted to make sure we weren't being followed or anything."

George didn't argue, but something was up. Justin was stretched as taut as a drum, and he was definitely more nervous than he'd been when they left. There hadn't been many people in town to recognize him, and the ones George had seen barely seemed to pay any mind to Justin. Something wasn't right, and he wondered if he should press the issue.

By the time they reached the driveway, Justin had slunk down in the seat and was staring straight ahead. He was slightly pale, and George wondered if he was sick or something. When they stopped, Justin helped him unload the purchases and haul them into the garage before going in the house without another word.

"What happened?" Ethan asked when George came in.

"I don't know."

"He went to his room and closed the door. Didn't say anything to either of us."

"I don't know," George repeated, his gaze trailing down the hall to the closed door. "He was acting funny in town but won't say why."

"Was he mobbed or something?"

"By the five people we saw? I don't think so." He ran through what happened and came up with nothing. "No one even said his name or anything. He left the hardware store and was looking at used clothes and watching the window."

Ethan shrugged. "We'll leave him alone and let him come out on his own. Something may have triggered something about the funeral."

"The funeral home did call on our way in and asked about hymns. He picked some, and we talked about forgiveness and things. Maybe I upset him." George told himself he needed to learn to keep his mouth shut.

"He's been holding on to his anger and hurt with his father like a security blanket. It's what keeps him going, in a way. When he has a tough role, he pulls out that pain, and it translates to the screen like nothing else. Everyone can feel it. So who knows? Maybe he is starting to let it go, and he doesn't know what to replace it with. Actors deal in emotion all the time, and maybe that anger has been what he built his craft on and now it's going away."

"Maybe," George said. He wasn't buying it. There was something else going on. The paleness and silence spoke of fear to George, but he wasn't sure if that was it. "Shit."

"What?"

"You said that there was something we didn't know about why Justin left. And he told me this morning that I didn't understand everything that happened."

"You think something triggered that?"

"I don't know. But it's possible. He acted more like a frightened rabbit than the Justin I knew or the one I've come to know again. I could be wrong, but I never pictured him as that type of person."

"He isn't," Ethan confirmed. "Justin is bold and strong. He has to be, or the sharks in Hollywood would eat him alive. Instead, he has his game, and they play it because everyone loves him. Justin doesn't have skeletons in his closet, and he never does stupid things like driving drunk or going out with underage boys. There's no shit to cover up. He's the real rags-to-riches story, and that's why they love him."

"So there has to be something that spooked him."

"It's possible that whoever he won't talk about is still in town. That monkey that's he's been carrying on his back could still be around. After all, he acquired the damn thing while he was here, so whatever happened has its roots here."

"We have to protect him from whatever it is. He's only here until the end of the week, and then he'll go back to Hollywood and he can resume his life."

Ethan chuckled nervously and shook his head. "I don't think so. Justin will go back to Hollywood, but if you think he'll be able to just go back to his life like nothing has happened...."

"His father is gone, and everything here will be settled."

"Please. I know what happened this morning, and I saw the goofy grin on his face. Justin has had a few affairettes, but nothing meaningful from his perspective. That changed this morning, and it's because of you. As I said, he'll go back to Hollywood, but I suspect nothing will be the same."

"He can't stay here," George said.

"Justin can do whatever he wants, but you're right. He has a life and a career that brings joy to millions."

"I'd never ask him to give that up. It was always his dream. He used to do all the shows in high school, and it was magical to watch him on stage. I used to get tickets to every performance just so I could sit in a dark theater and dream about what it must be like to do that. Justin and I have reconnected, but once the week is over, he and I will go our separate ways. I won't ask him to stay, and my life is here with my mom. Not that he's asked me to go there with him or anything." George figured he should clear that up just in case Ethan got the wrong idea.

"That's good to hear, because he has commitments, and if he tried to get out of them, they'd hand him his balls. His next movie is a smaller picture, but it could make his entire career. He's done action pictures, and if he can make this one a success, it will catapult him to the very top of the Hollywood ladder. It's an emotional film with incredible heart. But if he doesn't get back by Sunday and show up on Monday, there will be hell to pay."

"So we keep him quiet and out of sight as much as we can, let him get through the funeral, and at the end of the week, you'll take him back to Hollywood." George usually loved weekends, but not the one coming up. He wouldn't go back on his word, but he was finding it harder and harder to keep his word to everyone. He knew it was stupid to get his heart set on Justin, and he told himself that he'd gone into things with his eyes open, but he was in for a serious broken heart when Justin left. At least this time he'd see it coming.

GEORGE SPENT the rest of the afternoon helping his mother. Justin stayed in his room, and Ethan fretted. George took care of a few other questions from the funeral director. At dinnertime, Ethan got Justin, who had been asleep, and they had a quiet dinner, much simpler than the one the night before. Afterward they watched some television until after his mother went to bed. Ethan said good night, and then it was only him and Justin.

George felt much as he had the night before. He was so unsure of what Justin wanted that he was afraid to make any sort of move. He kept telling himself that this was Justin Grove, his old friend, but for some reason he kept feeling a little intimidated by Justin Hawthorne. Eventually, after sharing glances and awkwardness, George got up and said good night. He handed Justin the remote and went down the hall to the bathroom. He cleaned up and went to bed, leaving his door open partway.

"I can't read your mind," Justin said when he entered the room once George had climbed under the covers.

"I can't read yours either."

"So tell me what you want," Justin said. George rolled his eyes. "Okay, so I need to do the same." Justin lifted the covers and grinned. George hadn't worn anything to bed, and Justin shucked his clothes and climbed in with him. "It's been a while since I actually slept with anyone."

"We don't have to do anything but sleep if that's what you want." God, he hated how unsure he sounded. They'd had mind-blowing sex that morning, but now he was nervous as hell. What the heck was happening to him? He wasn't the most experienced guy in the world, but he was no shrinking violet either.

Justin tugged him close, lightly petting down his back. Damn, that was nice, and it added to the heat and inflamed him fast.

"Georgie, you never have to guess what I'm feeling because most of the time you know. I think that's what makes you so special."

"Ethan understands you," George countered.

"Maybe. But he doesn't…. I don't know. It's not the same. He doesn't know what it was like here and how hard it was for me to leave. I know I keep saying the same thing, but you have to know that I didn't want to go."

"Look, I told you that what happened made you the person you are. Well, I can't fault you, because it did the same for me. If you hadn't left, both our lives would be different. Maybe we'd still be here and happy or maybe we'd have made each other miserable and ended up hating each other. We'll never know."

"I guess not." Justin held him tight. "For the record, I'm sorry for the pain I caused you. But if it's any consolation, I was hurt just as badly."

Before George could muster any argument, Justin closed the last remaining distance between them and his lips were otherwise engaged. Not that George was complaining for an instant.

CHAPTER 5

JUSTIN HATED the thought of going to his father's funeral. He never thought he'd be here. The old goat was supposed to die and he would be thousands of miles away in the middle of a heavy shooting schedule, too busy to give it a second thought.

"The limousine will be here in a few minutes," Ethan told him when he stuck his head into the room. "You look good."

"You should think so. You packed it all," Justin said more grumpily than he intended.

"There's going to be press there. I suspect they will be quiet and off to the side, but they will be there." Ethan pushed his hands away and straightened his tie for him. "They know you and your dad had a falling out—no one has made a secret of that. But if they ask if you and your dad reconciled before his death, smile and hint that it's possible."

"God, the Hollywood spin on a funeral. Did Roy tell you to say that?" Justin demanded, and the sheepishness in Ethan's eyes told him he was right. "Jesus. Next time you talk to him about my personal life, tell him I said to fuck the hell off or so help me I'll kick his sanctimonious ass into next week." God, there were times he wanted to fire him, but Roy usually had good instincts, and Justin didn't need to explain the whole fight with his father yet again in some interview. He wanted that in the past.

"Don't get pissy. He was concerned, and he wasn't a dick about it at all. The guy really does care about you, and not just because you're a client."

Justin wasn't so sure about that, but he wasn't going to argue at the moment.

Ethan stepped back and looked him over. "You're ready to meet the public."

"You know I wanted to act and be famous, it was my goal, but I never understood how hard it was to be *on* all the time. Whenever I step out, I have to look exactly the way I want and be perfect and picture-ready. Most guys can wander out in a robe or something to get the paper or the mail, but I'll never be able to." He sighed softly.

"You have people to get the paper. Mainly me," Ethan said.

"You know what I mean. My life is hidden behind walls and other people. Sometimes I think I'm so inaccessible that I can't find myself." He smiled, and Ethan lightly smacked his chest. "I'm not kidding. There are agents, studios, publicists, bodyguards, all kinds of people between me and anyone in my life. My phone number is unlisted, and my house is in the name of a dummy corporation we set up so I could have a little privacy. Everything is built to keep me away from anyone who might get close enough to hurt me."

"It's also for your privacy. If that wasn't in place, you'd have people crawling through your bushes and rummaging through the trash."

"I know, but for a little while I'd like to be like everyone else."

"That ended with the Oscar nomination and People's Choice Awards. We all try to make it so you can lead as normal a life as possible," Ethan said.

Justin knew that, but it was still nice to be able to come and go and live normally, the way he had for the past few days. Granted, he knew that was going to come to an end very quickly. Once the funeral was over, the press would descend and try to dig up a story. He was really beginning to think he needed to leave earlier rather than later, but he hated to go and for only one reason—Georgie. He wanted to spend as much time with him as he could.

"We need to go," Ethan said.

They left the bedroom, meeting Shirley and George in the living room. Justin escorted them out to the limousine and waited until they were in before sitting on the very backseat, with Ethan next to him.

The driver backed out and drove the few miles to the funeral home. As Ethan had warned him, there were people milling around and a few news vans across the street. Justin tried to ignore them. When the car pulled to a stop, Ethan got out and held the door. Justin followed, waited for George and Shirley, and they all walked in together.

Justin was so damn nervous he could barely keep his feet under him. He knees shook as he made his way down the hall to the chapel. The casket was at the far side, lid open. It was wood colored, but from the shine, he thought it must have been metal. It looked comfortable enough as he approached the body of his father. "You were such a stubborn asshole," Justin muttered as he got closer. "I was different, and you couldn't handle it."

A lady had come up next to him, and her head snapped around to him. "Respect for the dead," she whispered.

Justin turned to her. "Bullshit. He's gone, and if he can hear me"—Justin made a pointed effort of looking toward the floor—"wherever he is, then he deserves an earful."

"You're his son?" she asked, and Justin nodded. "He was proud of you."

"How did you know him?"

"Your dad used to come to the senior center at the church a few times a week, and we got to know him." She turned, and Justin saw a group of older ladies sitting together. "He used to tell us all the things you were doing in Hollywood." She smiled a dentured grin. "He never stopped talking about you."

"Then why didn't he talk to me?" Justin asked. "If my father was so proud of me, he could have been part of my life if he might have called or talked to me. Instead there was nothing, and he was back here telling everyone about how proud of his son he was. That bastard had nothing to do with my success, and as for being proud of me, he did very little to make things that way. Unless throwing me to the wolves counts."

She sighed and turned back to his father's body. "There's no fool like an old fool." That seemed to say it all, and she patted Justin on the arm.

He turned back to the casket. "I wish things had been different," Justin said and turned away from where his father lay and sat down next to Ethan. Others came in slowly, talking in low tones. Justin paid little attention and only wished this whole thing was over. Finally the minister took his place and began the service.

Justin paid little attention. The casket lid had been closed, so he stared at it.

The minister read some scripture, and there were a few songs. "Jaime Grove was a tireless man," the minister said when it was time for the eulogy. "I had the pleasure of talking to a number of people these last few days, and I was astounded at his selflessness."

Justin raised his eyes, wondering if the minister had lost his mind.

"He worked at the church to help make repairs, and he spent hours helping out at our senior programs. Jaime was always there when we needed a hand. He used to drive people to doctor's appointments, and he took a group of ladies to the grocery store every week so they could do their shopping. Jaime never asked for a dime for any of it. He was just happy to help."

What the fuck? Justin looked around to find out if all this was true. He had to have his wires crossed. But the others in the room were nodding and seemed to agree. The minister went on to talk about Justin's family and how proud his father had been of him. He also talked a little about Justin's mother, and that was when it hit him. They were gone, and now he had a million questions he wanted to ask both of them, and he'd never be able to.

"Was my dad really like that?" Justin whispered to George.

"Yes. At least he seemed to have been before I knew him. Others were helping him by the time I came into the picture."

"I once asked him why he did all this, and the only answer he'd ever give was that he was trying to even the scale somehow," the minister added as he picked up on the theme and continued it through the remainder of his talk, which Justin barely heard.

His father had somehow turned into a decent human being, and Justin would never get to talk to him about it. The loss filled him, and Shirley took his hand, squeezing it lightly as he sat there trying not to look like a piece of his world had come crashing down around him.

The truth was that Justin had always hoped for some chance to reconcile with his parents. But his mother's death had taken half of that away, and now the rest was gone too. He would never get the chance to sit down and talk or for either of them to say that they had been wrong. Instead he was left alone and empty with nothing but a bunch of squandered chances. Justin sat staring. He wanted to get to know the person they were describing as his father. That person was completely different from the one he knew, the one who'd rejected him.

Justin hadn't known exactly what would be said at the funeral, but he had expected it to be less effusive and more general. To him, his father was the bastard who'd kicked him out, and he kept wondering why they didn't see that and why in the hell didn't the man who did things for everyone else have a big enough heart to have been able to accept that his only son, his only child, was different. This was massively unfair, and it had cost him his family.

Singing pulled him out of his thoughts, and he blinked a few times, expecting the cloud to dissipate, but it didn't. It sat over and around him, and he just let it. He was saying good-bye to his father and mother and what would never be between them, and as much as he wanted to deny it, he was having a tough time letting go. This entire funeral represented missed chances and opportunities for him and his parents.

The minister brought the funeral to an end. Justin sat in his place while the others stood and quietly filed out. He couldn't move. George stood next to him, with Ethan and Shirley doing the same. "Please take them back to the car," Justin told Ethan and slowly stepped toward the casket.

His legs felt like lead, and his feet hardly left the floor, but he made the few steps to where his father lay and slowly lifted the lid, looking down on his father's face for the last time.

"You were an asshole to me, and I'd call you a son of a bitch, but I liked Grandma too much for that. You wasted what time we could have had together, and you managed to take Mom away from me and cut me off even when she died. You ripped away my family because you didn't understand that I was being who I was, and you had trouble accepting that." Justin stared at his father's lifeless body and wanted to shake him. "You could tell everyone how fucking proud of me you were, but that changes nothing. You were proud of someone you sent away." Justin swallowed and closed his eyes when he felt Georgie's hand on his back.

"We can go when you're ready."

Justin nodded and continued looking at his father. "I'll be out in a minute." George left him. "So this is it. You're in a box, and this is the last time I'll set eyes on you. I hope you're with Mom and that you realize what you did. But I can't keep holding on to this crap any longer. I have my own life and people who care about me. I've made mistakes, and so have you. But it's over—the fight, the hurt, the resentment. It has to end." Justin sighed and closed the lid before turning away and joining George, Ethan, and Shirley where they waited near the exit. The limousine pulled up, and the people who'd lingered watched as he climbed inside. The others joined him inside, and then Justin sat back, closed his eyes, and breathed deeply. It was over, and he felt lighter than he had in a long time.

"Did you make peace with what happened?" Ethan asked.

"I think so. The past is the past, and I'm letting it go." He sighed once again and then smiled slightly. "Where are we going now?"

"To the lunch," Shirley said. "The church I go to has set one up. I suspect it's going to be well attended because everyone is going to want to see you. They'll be respectful and nice. I know that."

God, he hoped so. Just for the rest of the day, he wanted to be able to be Justin Grove. He didn't want to have to be on or entertain people. He needed some time to be alone with his thoughts.

TWO HOURS later, after talking to everyone and trying not to seem tired and drawn, Justin was finally able to leave the church. He went to use the restroom and bumped into someone. Justin said excuse me, grumbling under his breath that he needed to watch where he was going.

"I heard you were back in town."

The deep rumbling voice was all too familiar, the one he heard in his nightmares. Justin backed away. The sneer on Mark's lips when Justin looked at him was more than reminiscent.

"Yes," Justin said as he stepped to the side to go around him. "Just for the funeral." He needed to get the hell out of here. Justin forced his legs to move forward as Mark jostled his shoulder. Justin picked up the pace, stepped into the bathroom, and closed the door, leaning against it as he breathed deeply. His legs held, but damn if he didn't feel like a kid again.

The door had a lock on the inside, and Justin threw it and went to the sink. He completely forgot why he'd come in here in the first place and had to stop the heat from rising to his face. Justin had known he'd run into that bastard. He'd managed to stay away from him when he'd been in town, but why was the fucker at his father's funeral? Justin balled his hands into fists and shook all over.

It took a few minutes for him to calm down, and then Justin used the bathroom and washed his hands. He didn't want to leave in case Mark was still out there, and yet he wasn't particularly interested in hiding in the bathroom for the rest of the day. In the end, he unfastened the lock and pulled open the door as hard as he could, ready to run for it.

Ethan stood outside looking at him like he'd lost his mind. "What happened? Did you fall in?" Then Ethan turned back to Mark as though they'd been talking. Fucking hell, he needed to figure out a way to separate those two. The last thing he needed was Ethan and Mark becoming chummy.

Justin's mouth hung open for a second. He ignored Ethan's question and snapped, "We need to go," more angrily than he intended, but he knew Ethan would get ready. He then went to find George and Shirley, who were saying good-bye to friends, and they headed out to the limousine. He was more than ready to go back to George's and do something mindless like watch television.

George and Shirley got in behind him, and eventually Ethan joined them and closed the door.

"Thank goodness that's over," Justin said, pulling off his tie. "It was a nice service and everything. Thank you both for arranging it."

"You're welcome, sweetheart," Shirley said.

"I saw you talking to Mark Bobb," George said. "Justin and I went to school with him. His father is the mayor, has been for twenty years or so now."

"He was always a dick in high school," Justin said.

George chuckled softly. "I don't think he's changed much. He's a contractor, and I swear if his dad wasn't throwing work his way, he'd starve."

"Good to know," Ethan said.

They arrived at the house, went inside, and flopped onto the sofa.

"We can go out to dinner when it comes time," Shirley said as she took off her coat and draped it over one of the living room chairs. "I don't know about the rest of you, but I'm tired." As she sat down, the light coming in the window dimmed. Justin looked out as the rain started. It had been threatening all day. Rain and dreary low clouds seemed to fit the mood of the day.

George turned on the television, but Justin ignored it, continuing to watch the rain come down. "Have you made arrangements for our return trip?" Justin asked Ethan. "I think we need to go back on Saturday. That will give us a day in LA before I have to report for shooting." He hated the thought of going back, and yet he knew it was inevitable.

"Should I make a hotel reservation in Baltimore for Friday night?" Ethan asked as he got up. Justin knew he was already getting his computer to complete the arrangements. He didn't even have to look.

"You're welcome to stay here. You know that," George said.

"Thank you." He turned, and George stood next to him, sliding his hand into Justin's. Part of him wanted to tell Ethan to make the hotel reservation. It would be easier to simply say good-bye than drag it out, but the other part wanted to stay until the last possible second.

"I can get a flight at 2:05 p.m., so whatever you want to do will work."

George stepped closer, squeezing his fingers lightly.

"We'll leave Saturday morning," Justin said. It would give him one more night with George before he had to go, and those were turning out to be very precious.

"We're all set," Ethan said and continued working with the computer on his lap as he watched whatever was on television.

"What are you doing now?" Justin questioned.

"Checking messages. There's a company that will be coming tomorrow at four to pick up your father's car. They're going to ship it to LA for you, and it should arrive on Wednesday, or a week from today."

"Are you serious about the rest?" George asked.

"Yeah. Take anything that you'd like, donate all the medical equipment, and then sell the rest and we'll donate the money." It would benefit others, and he certainly didn't need it. "This way it will do someone some good."

"Okay," George said and leaned closer. Justin was grateful that there was no one out in front of the house. He didn't want to move, but he also didn't want pictures taken through the window. He deserved his privacy, as did George.

"I'm tired, Georgie," Justin whispered.

"Then go lie down. No one is going to blame you for taking a nap after this afternoon."

Justin sighed. "I mean I'm *tired*. I didn't realize how tired until I got the chance to slow down. I've done film after film, and I have the next two or three contracted, I can't really remember. They're stretching out like a road in front of me." He turned to see if either of the others was paying them any attention. Shirley was engrossed in the television and Ethan in his screen. "I know it's what I need to do, but my energy levels feel so low, and all I want is some time to relax and put my feet up."

"You have a couple days before you go back. Just do that. I know it isn't a long time, but I was thinking we could go out for a drive tomorrow. It's supposed to be sunny. We could drive to the battlefield, get out and see some monuments, explore a little. No one will pay us any mind, and it'll be quiet. This time of the year, everything there is just waking up."

Justin nodded. "That sounds so nice. Ethan will have our car so he can go wherever he wants."

"Do you think he'll be angry or feel left out?"

"I'll be fine," Ethan said, and when Justin turned, Ethan flashed him a smile before going back to his computer screen. Justin shrugged and turned back to George.

"How do you get used to a near complete lack of privacy?" George asked.

"You just do. You remember when I did that nude scene where they showed my ass? Well, everyone on set saw my stuff because I was, in essence, naked, and while the camera didn't show anything, it was pretty much on display for everyone else. You turn it off and do the job. After a while you don't notice that the people you trust are around you." He glanced at Ethan, who was once again absorbed in his computer screen.

"I don't know if I could get used to it."

"It's hard to explain. There are hair people and makeup people in the morning. Costumers and wardrobe people who fit and sometimes help me change because some of the costumes can be so intricate. Then there are directors, camera operators, assistants, and the assistants of some of the assistants. It takes a lot of people to make a movie production go smoothly. At home I'm exhausted, so I let Ethan, Roy, and a few others help me with my life so I can continue working and not have to worry about things like dishes and laundry, or paying the light bill."

"It seems you have a life full of people," George said. "I'm glad you aren't lonely."

"I never said that. You can be completely alone in a room full of people." Justin spent all day around dozens of people but was pretty much alone. Ethan was the one person he knew in LA who truly cared about him. "It happens all the time." He leaned against George and tried to let it all go. He had a couple of days left, and George was right—he needed to make the best of them before he returned to his own version of the grindstone.

CHAPTER 6

WHY WAS it that when you were having fun, the time flew by, and when things were going badly, the clock seemed to run in slow motion? For George the next couple of days went by in the blink of an eye. He and Justin went to Gettysburg and walked all over the battlefields. They saw scores of monuments, climbed to the top of the Pennsylvania one for the view, and surprisingly enough, had a chance to be alone. The day was sunny but cold and windy. They'd buttoned up, so they hadn't minded the wind as they stood together, but it seemed most everyone else must have. That was fine with them.

George spent some time arranging the cleanout of Justin's dad's house, and the agency he worked for gladly took the medical equipment and immediately found uses for it with people in need. That had made Justin smile when George told him.

God, that smile. No wonder he was famous, because every time Justin threw one of those in his direction, George's belly clenched and it seemed like the air around him warmed, like Justin was his own private sun. "I love when you do that," George said as they rode back from Harrisburg on Friday afternoon.

"What?" Justin asked.

"Relax and smile. It means you've been able to let go for a while." He remembered those same smiles from before Justin had left. They had tended to be few and far between, just like now. He hated doing anything to make them disappear. But he felt he had to.

"I was wondering if we could stop at the diner for a couple pieces of their pie before we go home," Justin said.

"Pie?" George asked. "My, my. Mr. 'I need to watch my weight because the camera adds ten pounds' wants to stop for pie?" He did his best imitation of a fainting Southern belle. Granted, he was driving, so it wasn't much.

"Don't give up your day job," Justin teased. "Today is our last day, so I thought I'd try to make it a little special."

"Pie sounds nice," George agreed, and they continued along the country road, approaching the town of Biglerville. He'd missed his chance to ask the question that had been burning at him all day, and he was running out of time. Maybe the universe was telling him that it was best that he let it lie. It had happened years earlier, and while George needed to know why Justin had left, Justin didn't want to talk about it at all, no matter how many times George tried to bring it up.

George parked the car in front of the diner.

"Why don't we just go home?" Justin asked with a hint of something that sent a chill up George's spine.

There was fear in Justin's voice, and George scanned around them. The diner appeared nearly empty except for one person sitting at a table in one of the windows. "What's going on?"

"I'm just not very hungry, I guess," Justin said, looking anywhere but at the diner.

"There something interesting out your side window?" George asked as Justin turned away and finally looked at the diner. Hatred flashed on his face for a few seconds before Justin covered it, but it was clear enough to George. "You're going to have to tell me what has you running so scared." George put the car in park and turned off the engine, crossing his arms over his chest.

"Let's just go home," Justin said more forcefully.

George knew he was probably being a little mean and pushing too hard, but he wasn't going to give up. "I'm going to get some pie and ice cream. You can stay here in the car if you want, but I'm going inside."

"No!" Justin snapped and grabbed George's arm when he went to open the door.

"Then tell me what's going on."

"I'm not going anywhere near him."

"Who—Mark?" George blinked as some pieces clicked into place. "Is that why you took off out of the hardware store the other day and why you were hiding in the bathroom after the funeral?" George had definitely noticed his departure and the fact that he was in the bathroom for a very long time. "What the hell happened?"

"Let's just go home," Justin said half under his breath.

George started the engine and backed out of the spot as he saw Mark turn in their direction. Even through the window, George saw the menace being sent back their way. George checked his mirrors and then pulled into traffic and out of town. He had no intention of letting Justin off the hook, but first he had to get him calmed down.

Justin's hands shook most of the rest of the ride to the house. He went right inside, and when George followed, he found Ethan in a flurry of activity, grabbing suitcases. "What's going on?"

Ethan shrugged. "His Highness just pronounced that we're leaving in ten minutes and practically kicked me in the ass to get everything packed and loaded. What happened?"

George shook his head as anger welled up from old hurts deep inside. "Ignore him," George said. "The bastard isn't going to do this to me twice." He charged down the hall and into the bedroom. Justin was throwing a stack of shirts into a suitcase. "You coward!"

"Don't think I'm going to rise to your bait." Justin continued packing.

"I'm not baiting you. I'm telling the truth. You're a coward, and just like back then, you're running like some scared rabbit." All Justin did was growl without stopping his packing. "Something has you so scared that you'll run like a little girl, and you don't even think I deserve some sort of explanation." George's anger continued to grow, but he kept his temper in check.

"This has nothing to do with you," Justin said, slamming a pair of pants into the suitcase.

"It doesn't? You left me all those years ago, and you're doing the same thing now. So either you're running from something or I've done something to drive you away, just like seven years ago. Don't you think I deserve to know what it is?" George pressed. Ethan took a step into the room, and George turned to him with fire in his eyes. Ethan stopped and then backed out of the room. "I've had more than enough of this bullshit." He grabbed the suitcase and dumped the contents on the floor. "Now you can start over."

"Asshole!"

"Scaredy-cat! Chickenshit!"

Justin snatched up the suitcase. "Fucktard!"

"Butthead!" George countered, knocking the suitcase back on the floor. "I can do this all day. So you aren't going to get anywhere until you tell me what's really going on. What has you so scared you'll run away with your tail between your legs?"

George waited, watching as the air and steam went out of Justin like a balloon. His hands stilled, and then he stood quietly in the middle of the room. "I need to go, okay?"

"No. It's not okay. You can't run from whatever it is you're trying to get away from."

"How do you know?" Justin challenged.

"Because our fears and memories go with us wherever we go. They don't stay in one place. You know that."

"No. But…." He turned to him. "I can't, Georgie."

"The only way to lessen whatever has gotten hold of you is to talk about it. You need to get it into the open so you can deal with it, instead of holding it inside." George sat on the side of the bed, trying to seem less imposing and threatening. "I'm on your side, Jus. I always was, but I can't help if I don't know what's hurting you."

"No one can help, and that's a fact."

"I'm not so sure about that," George told him. "I used to keep all kinds of secrets from my mom and dad. I didn't tell them about you and me until all that stuff with your dad, and you know what? They were there for me. They said that you could stay with us because I asked them. That's all I did. I asked, and they said yes. They weren't going to let you live on the street, and they knew how I felt about you."

Justin turned toward him, a single tear running down his cheek. "Don't you think I wanted to stay? I could have had the life I always wanted with you." Justin turned away. "But if I'd stayed, then you'd have been in danger, and I couldn't allow that to happen. I had to go. There was no other choice." Justin stepped around the pile of clothes on the floor and sat next to him.

"You need to explain that, Justin." He took his hand.

"I… can't," Justin said without any of the heat from before.

George sat quietly and waited, hoping that Justin would open up.

"You have to," George said.

"Because you want me to?"

"No." He gently stroked the back of Justin's hand. "Because whatever you've been holding inside is eating you alive. This is where you grew up and where a lot of people know you. You're like the town hero in a way, yet you're afraid to go into the diner for pie."

Justin shivered and leaned closer. George put his arm around Justin's shoulders and held him. They sat in silence for a good five minutes, hearing only the sounds of cooking drifting down the hall.

"You know I came here after my dad threw me out, and I had to go to work that night," Justin said. "It was the only way I was going to make some money."

"I know. You were at the Dairy Whip."

"Yeah. I had to close it that night, and I was working with Jane Peterson, but her boyfriend showed up a little before eleven, so I told her to go and finished the cleanup myself. There wasn't much left to do, and customers had stopped coming a half hour earlier. I locked everything up, set the alarm, and left to go to the car. You remember that old thing I was driving?"

"Yeah. What happened to it?"

"The car made it as far as the outskirts of Chicago before it died forever and I started figuring out other ways to get where I needed to go. Thankfully I had saved enough, and bus tickets were pretty cheap."

"God."

"Yeah. Looking back, I'm surprised I made it at all, and I was damn lucky I met Ethan when I arrived." Justin grew quiet. "The thing is, that night, I didn't make it to my car right away. There was someone waiting for me."

"Mark?" George asked.

Justin nodded. "He grabbed me and threw me on the ground." Justin's voice broke. "He held my hands and shoved something in my mouth. He kept saying things like he'd heard all about me, and that he was going to give me exactly what I wanted." Justin shook hard.

George clamped his eyes shut. "Oh God," he whispered.

"Yeah. When he was done, he said that I better not tell anyone. Then he changed his mind and said I should leave town or else he'd wait around for you. He said he'd do the same thing to you." Justin broke down, burying his face in George's shirt. "I couldn't have that."

"But…. What he did…."

"No one was going to believe me. I was a kid, and Mark was the son of the mayor. My mom and dad didn't want me, so why would anyone believe anything I said? I was just the fag kid in town, and I had to protect you. If I stayed, I knew he'd go after you because I was living with you."

"How did you know he'd leave me alone when you left?"

"Because he didn't know about you specifically. He said that anyone I got my fag hands on would pay. If I was around you, I knew he'd put things together and come after you. I couldn't have you hurt. My stuff was already in the back of the car, so I pulled up my pants and got into the car and drove. I could barely see for hours, there were so many tears in my eyes. I ended up sleeping in the car beside the road when I couldn't stay awake anymore. I had no idea where I was going to go, and when the car died, I just took what I could carry. I only had two old suitcases of stuff anyway. I managed to make it to a garage, but the engine was blown, and the guy gave me a hundred bucks for the car as parts and a ride to the bus station."

"My God," George muttered.

"Yeah, and every minute took me farther from you. I thought about calling you to say where I was. More than once I started to dial your number, but what was I going to do? You were safe with me gone, and that was what mattered."

Now it was George's turn to shake like a leaf. "You just left instead of coming to me?"

"I couldn't let him hurt you, Georgie. You were all I had left, and yeah, I wasn't in the same place, but I knew you were safe and that you had your mom and dad. I didn't want you getting kicked out too, or hurt, so it was best I went somewhere else. California seemed like a good idea. I was a gay kid, and I'd heard all kinds of stories that California had lots of other gay people. My plan was to get settled, and then I could send for you. But that was dumb. What was I going to do? Especially after what I realized I'd done once my head cleared and I could think straight. By then I was in LA, and Ethan had helped me get a job." Justin turned to look at him. "I never stopped thinking about you, Georgie. Every day I wished and dreamed of you, but as time went on.... It seemed dumber and dumber for me to call, so I didn't. I got up the courage to send you a letter the one time."

"And it had some bullshit return address. All I knew when I got it was that you were in California. I had no idea how to get in touch with you. So I tried to go on, but it didn't work, and then, son of a bitch, I saw you in a movie. At least I knew you were still alive."

"Sometimes I didn't feel like it, but I was busy, and I tried to put what happened behind me. But it was hard."

"Did you talk to anyone?" George asked.

Justin shook his head.

"No one?"

"Nope. The only person I've ever told is you, just now."

George's fists clenched. "So help me God, the next time I see Mark Bobb, I'm going to beat the living shit out of him."

"No you're not, because he's an asshole, but I have nothing on him. There's no evidence of what he did, and his dad is still mayor."

"But people will listen to you," George said.

"It doesn't matter. That's in the past, like the rest of it. My dad is dead, and Mark doesn't matter much anymore. I'll be going back to California tomorrow, and he'll still be here." Justin rested his head on George's shoulder once again. "At least you know that you didn't do anything wrong."

"You...." George turned to him. "Stupid ass. I would have stood by you, and so would my mom and dad. There's no excuse for him to

103

have… for him to do that to you or anyone. That slimy, sick son of a bitch. I want to rip the bastard to pieces." Now that he knew the whole story, he was seeing red and shaking with nearly uncontrolled anger. "That asshole took you away from me, and you let him."

"Georgie," Justin said, "that's not helping. I knew you'd act this way. That was part of the reason I never told you. I've had to live with it and have dealt with it."

"Bullshit. You were shaking in the car just from seeing him."

"Yeah, well. It was years ago, and I have no intention of letting him get close to me again. As you said, I can't keep holding on to everything, so I have to get past it."

"I meant your dad. Not the piece of shit who… who…." George found the word caught in his throat, and it wouldn't come out. "I want to fucking kill him."

"I know. I used to think about doing that too. So many times I thought I'd come back and I'd be famous and he'd be a useless sack of shit."

"Well, you are famous, and he is completely useless."

"Yeah. But I feel so different, and then I met you again, and every time I see the fucker, I keep hearing his threat over and over. I thought it would be different, but it's the shits. So…."

"You were going to leave again."

"I have to go tomorrow morning anyway."

"Yes. But we still have one more night." George sounded dumb even to his own ears. They had just talked about what Mark had done to Justin, and George's mind was now on sex. It was doubtful that Justin would want to do anything. Hell, how could Justin ever have had sex again?

"I can tell what you're thinking," Justin said softly. "You're wondering how I can be intimate with anyone after what Mark did. But what he did was about control and violence, causing pain. It had nothing to do with sex. It was about making me feel terrible about myself, and he did that for a long time. I still sometimes have trouble telling people I'm gay, though most people know by now. The thing is, when I have to tell someone, I still get this unsettled, ralphy feeling in my stomach, and I think about what Mark did to me and wonder if the person in front of me is going to try to hurt me."

"Justin...." George groaned and tried to get his mind around what he'd been told. "I'm so sorry for all of it. Especially that he hurt you. I'd kick his ass to next month if I thought you'd let me."

"He's not worth it," Justin told him gently. "So I'm afraid of him—can you blame me?"

"No."

"But at least he can't hurt me again, because I won't let him. I never want to be in the same place as him, but I can take away his power and his ability to hurt me." Justin's jaw set firmly. "I take it away. He has no power over me any longer."

"Is it that simple?" George asked. It couldn't possibly be. If it were, then every victim would easily be able to get past what happened to them.

Justin chuckled. "Of course not. But acting teaches us that half the battle is the right costume and makeup to get you in the frame of mind. If you look like Henry VIII, then you start to act like you think he'd act. So saying the words is the beginning of making it a reality. It's a start, but no more." Justin leaned closer and lightly kissed George's neck. "What happened had nothing to do with sex or what I feel for you."

"But everything... you...." He was mumbling because his thoughts refused to settle down.

"Yes, I went through a lot, some of it reminiscent of hell, but in a way it brought me back to you, at least for a while." Justin paused. "I already know your answer, but I want to ask anyway. My career is in Hollywood, and well... I can't stay here. I know your life is here, and so is your mother's, but...."

"You're asking me to come with you," George supplied.

"Yes. I already know it isn't fair of me to expect you to uproot and move your life clear across the country. But I want you to know that you'd make me happy and that I'd do my best to make you happy."

George's heart fluttered with joy. "I...."

"Like I said, I already knew your answer. You have a life here, and a good one. You have friends and family, a career you love, and—" Justin stopped for a second. "I know it's stupid of me to even ask, except I want you to know that I want you. That I'll always want you." He tugged George into a hug. "You need to find someone who will love you for all the incredible things that you are."

"But what if I love you?" George asked, unable to hold in the words.

"And I love you enough to understand that I have to let you go. We've known each other again for a week. Picking up and ruining your life for me isn't something I can let you do."

"Let me?" George said more loudly than he intended. "Who says I'd want to?" George added much more lightly, his own voice as fragile as the thinnest glass. "God, Jus, things just don't seem to work out for us, do they?"

"No. But it doesn't matter," Justin sputtered. "I mean, it does matter, because I want you with me, but it isn't like it's going to change the feelings I have for you. They've been with me for seven years now, and they're not going anywhere." He tugged him down, gently bringing their lips together.

"So you asked me to come with you... so I'd know that you want me?" George asked.

"Yes. Because I do. More than anything." The hope in Justin's eyes was so enticing, so magnetic, that George was seconds away from agreeing. He even opened his mouth to say yes and then laughter drifted in, Ethan and his mother joking and having a good time. He couldn't do that to her. The phone rang, and he heard his mother pick it up. Ethan's voice went quiet, but his mother's filled with her usual happiness as she chattered on with whoever had called. He couldn't leave her alone here, and moving her to California would take her away from everyone and everything she knew. The thought died on his lips, and he clamped them closed. Justin had been right, even if George hadn't wanted him to be.

George sighed. "I want to be with you too. But I can't leave Mom, and I won't rip her away from the people she knows."

Justin nodded slowly.

"So what do we do?"

"We say good-bye tomorrow, but this time I promise I'll do a better job of keeping in touch with you."

"Better? You didn't at all."

"I didn't say the bar was set particularly high. But you have my private cell number, and few other people do, and I know how to call you. I was thinking that maybe you could come for a visit sometime."

"Yeah, I'd like that," George said, but he wasn't sure any visit would actually happen. Once they went their separate ways, it might be best if they went on with their lives. They'd had these few days together, and there were still some precious hours before they were parted once again. "Maybe when you have some time in your schedule you can let me know, and I can take some time off."

Justin leaned in closer, kissing him once again. "I don't think I'll ever get enough of that… of you."

"You're going to have to," George said and closed his eyes as a wave of longing washed over him. He could wish all he wanted, but things were the way they were. "Sometimes I wish that things could be easier."

"My mom always said that anything that came easy wasn't worth having." Justin scooted closer. "If that's the case, then you are definitely worth having, because so little between us has come easily." Justin gently pushed George back on the bed, the energy between them rising by the second.

"Dinner will be ready in a little while," his mother called down the hall.

"It's not dinnertime yet," Justin said.

George stroked Justin's cheek. "That's my mother's way of telling us to behave. We'll have all night together."

Justin slowly got up, staring at him. "Damn, I love the sight of you in bed." He didn't look away, watching, scanning. Heat welled quickly in George's belly, and he was tempted to push the door closed and say to hell with what his mother knew and take Justin right then. That temptation rose as Justin continued staring at him.

"What are you doing?"

"Memorizing you," Justin answered. "I want to remember the depth in your eyes and the way your lips curve right at the top. I will not forget how you taste or how you feel against me for as long as I live. I know that for a fact."

"I'm just me," George said. "I'm not all that."

"Then you need to take a closer look in the mirror." Justin stalked nearer. "You're everything."

He swallowed, and George watched his throat work, mesmerized by the enticing motion.

"It's so much easier to believe the bad things or what's disappointing than the good things, and you definitely are one of the best."

"I can't believe you have to leave," George said and instantly wished he hadn't. He'd known all week that Justin was going to have to return to California, and he'd honestly thought he'd be able to take it. But it was turning out to be so much harder than he ever thought.

"Georgie," Justin said softly.

George knew that Justin was just as broken up as he was. "I know. I went into this with my eyes open, but you can't blame me for being sad about it."

Justin bent to pick up the clothes that George had strewn all over the floor earlier. George couldn't help it; he whistled softly.

"Are you whistling at my ass?" Justin asked as he straightened up and placed the clothes on the bed.

"Of course I am. It's a world-class ass, and half the women and every gay man in the country would give anything to have the view I have right now." George grabbed Justin's butt, and he jumped a little. He stood and pressed to Justin's backside, holding him close. "You're really warm."

"And you're hot." Justin took one of his hands and brought it to his lips, kissing it lightly. "I want to remember all of you."

"Me too." George rested his head against Justin's shoulders and let his eyes drift closed as he breathed deeply, inhaling Justin's musk. His head swam, and he groaned softly. His body reacted, and he knew Justin could feel it. He was beyond being coy at this point. George wanted Justin to know the effect he had on him. "We should go make sure Ethan and my mother aren't spilling both our secrets."

"Like what?" Justin asked, turning in George's arms. "I already know about the time you had an accident in second grade and when you lost a tooth and thought they were all going to fall out at once." Justin smiled. "I remember the time you ate too many cherries at summer camp and puked all over the counselor."

Justin was trying not to laugh, and George wanted to slap him.

"Yeah, but I bet Ethan knows things that I don't." George released Justin and turned to the door. He was about to take off when Justin grabbed him. He twisted out of Justin's grasp and raced down the hall toward the kitchen. He bolted around the table and sat next to Ethan, with Justin right behind him.

"Don't you say a word," Justin growled at Ethan.

"About what?" Ethan asked.

"I want some stories about Justin, preferably embarrassing ones," George said. "He has plenty of them on me."

Ethan did his best to look innocent. "I don't have any."

"See?" Justin said, pulling out a chair.

"Wait, there's the one where he went into an audition and was so nervous he nearly fell off the stage. Or how about the time he was called from the bathroom and walked into the audition with toilet paper stuck to his shoes?"

"Perfect. There has to be something better. Is there any truth to the rumor that he had a three-way with a set of twins?" George asked. He knew it wasn't possible. That wasn't at all the Justin he knew.

"The tabloids will print anything. Though some of the stories are hilarious to read. Apparently Justin is the oldest son of Bigfoot. His mother had a thing for really hairy men and said what the hell when she was on a trip to the Northwest."

They all laughed at that one.

"One story said that I had plastic surgery a month before I had to do my nude scene to have the fat sucked out of my ass." He stood and turned around. "Does this look like I've had any fat sucked out of it?"

"No," George said, swatting at Justin's butt. "It looks to me like someone has a thing for his ass and likes showing it off to everyone."

"I do not," Justin protested.

"Really?" George continued. "Show of hands. How many people in this room have had their bare butt filmed for all to see?" George was teasing, but he damn near choked when his mother raised her hand. Justin and Ethan nearly fell over in their mirth. "Mother!"

"Do tell," Ethan said.

"I wasn't always this old, and I was wild in my youth." She got up and brushed by Justin, who was holding the back of one of the chairs. "I'm going to start dinner."

"What did you do?" Ethan prodded. "I bet you knocked their socks off. Did you do a movie that scandalized everyone?"

"No, I posed nude for an artist. This was before I met George's father. The artist was something else, and I was in New York for a few weeks. He saw me and asked if I'd pose. Of course I wasn't sure, but my friend said she'd go with me, and then he asked me to pose without my clothes. I was shocked! And titillated," she added, and George wanted the floor to open up and swallow him.

"Come on, Georgie," Justin said as he sat down next to him, gently taking his hand. "This is cool."

"She's not your mother," he said.

"Go ahead, Shirley. What happened?"

"He painted my picture and paid me. He was a real gentleman and didn't try anything. But damn, I wish he had. Those eyes were magnificent, and his hair was black, with waves. He was meltingly hot but apparently liked his bed partners of the male variety. Lord knows I tried," she added coyly, looking up at the ceiling. "Anyway, that's where it ended. I left, and he had his painting." She turned toward the stove.

"Where is the painting now?" Justin asked.

She smiled. "It's hanging in the Guggenheim, or at least it was."

George nearly fell off his chair. "Why didn't you ever tell me this before?"

"It never came up, dear. Your father knew, of course. We went to visit it a few times, and it always got his motor running." Damn it, she was laughing at him. "I know you don't see me as anything but an old lady, but I'm not just that." She banged a pot on the stove.

George stood and went to her. "It's just that you're my mother, and you're supposed to be perfect and…."

"I am perfect, and I have a painting that proves it," she added. "Just because I'm not twentysomething any longer doesn't mean I'm dried up and useless. Yes, sometimes I have trouble remembering things, but I still had a life, and I wasn't always Miss Goody Two-Shoes."

"I think that's pretty obvious," George said and hugged her. "God, Mom, I love you."

"And I love you too." She patted his cheek. "Now I need to get started or we're not going to get any dinner." She turned away, and George joined the others. If she wanted help, she'd ask, but mostly it was a "get out of the way" type of thing when she cooked.

"I have our flights confirmed and our seats," Ethan said. "If we leave before seven in the morning, we should be fine. I called Roy to keep him from having a heart attack, and we're all set. So all we have to do is pack."

Justin nodded, but he didn't say anything. George sat back down, and Justin held his hand under the table. It seemed like Justin didn't want him too far away, and George was fine with that. They talked and helped his mother with dinner for the next hour or so. Once the food was on the table, they ate in relative quiet. For George, each hour brought them closer to morning, when Justin had to leave.

Justin's phone rang as they were starting to clean up. He left the room to take the call and returned storming. "That was Roy. The director wants me on set Sunday instead of Monday."

"We'll be home," Ethan said, "but you're going to be exhausted."

"That's just it. He wants me on location in Lake Arrowhead on Sunday." He was so tense his hair stood up a little.

"What did you say?" Ethan asked. He seemed to know what to do to help with the situation. George was completely useless and kept his distance, letting them talk.

"I didn't. He said to get a flight as soon as possible, but I don't want to fly all night."

George's stomach plummeted as he realized he was probably going to say good-bye to Justin earlier than he expected. He caught Justin's eye and shrugged before turning away. He didn't want him to see his expression. George wanted one last night together, but he wasn't going to stand in Justin's way.

"I have to call him back," Justin said and then left the room. Ethan seemed resigned to whatever they had to do and had his computer ready. "We have arrangements…," drifted in from the other room. "We'll be home tomorrow." The tiredness that had slipped out of Justin's voice over the last few days was back in a big way. "Roy, you tell him that I'll be there on Monday as originally planned. If he's not happy, remind him that I'm not either, and that he needs to stick with his commitments. I don't break mine, and I expect him to keep his." There was quiet for a few seconds. "You can call me back if you like, but it doesn't matter. I'll be on that plane tomorrow, and I'm not showing up until Monday."

Justin returned and handed his phone to Ethan.

"What are you doing?"

"Putting a layer between me and Roy."

"It's a game of sorts," Ethan said, picking up the phone when it rang. "Hey, Roy," he said and listened. "We're still in Biglerville, and you ask him if he wants his star with bags under his eyes or with energy and ready to work. Also tell him that Justin was here for his father's funeral. We can play that to the hilt and make him look like the biggest ass on earth… and we will. Now, just so we're clear. We are not changing our schedule at all. We're flying home tomorrow, and Justin will be on set Monday morning."

Ethan was so reasonable, and Justin sighed next to George, holding his hand tightly.

"Look, Roy, we're getting tired of going around and around with this. Just tell him no. Earn some of that percentage you're paid and grow a set of balls." Ethan groaned.

"He tells him that all the time. It's a joke between them," Justin said. "Right now Roy is sputtering and calling Ethan every name in the book, and then he's going to give in and make Ethan promise that I'll be there on Monday."

Sure enough, that was exactly what happened. "See you Monday," Ethan said and hung up.

"What was that all about?" George asked.

"Most likely a nervous agent and a director trying to add pressure. They know where Justin is, and they're trying to make sure that we understand the schedule."

"Also the director was trying to show he was top dog," Justin said, his expression firming. "But I'm top dog, and now he knows it."

"I see," George said, not understanding this at all.

"It's a game of who's going to blink first and who can get what they want," Ethan explained. "He and I have gotten good at playing it. Roy is in our corner, but he's nervous. He'd be much happier if Justin was in LA sitting by the pool."

"This whole thing is weird. People travel all the time," George said.

"Yeah, they do. But they get nervous when someone they're paying a lot of money isn't where they can see them. I know it's goofy, but it's true. They'll settle down, and I'll call Roy once we're at the airport. Now, let's not worry about this anymore."

"Hallelujah to that," Shirley said and opened the freezer door. "I have ice cream."

"I'm going to have to go on a diet for weeks after this trip," Justin said with a smile.

"You'll need the energy for later," George whispered to him, and Justin groaned and nodded, his eyes darkening almost instantly.

His mother got some bowls. "I have chocolate, mint chip, and strawberry, as well as vanilla."

"Are you opening an ice cream parlor, Mom?" George asked.

His mother rolled her eyes at him and began scooping. By the time she had everything back in the freezer, each of them had a huge bowl and they were well on their way to sugar shock. It was awesome, even with the sword of Damocles hanging over them.

THE EVENING was subdued for the most part. They were all full and ended up in the living room. The conversation died away, and George felt Justin pulling into himself. Not that George could blame him—he was doing the same thing. They sat together on the sofa, watching reruns of *NCIS*. Well, that was on the television, but George wasn't really watching. He leaned against Justin and tried not to fall into depression. They only had a few hours and then things would be like they had been before Justin had come back into his life. His mother kept sending looks his way, and he knew what she thought. His mother loved Justin, but she had warned him that this could happen, and he hadn't listened.

George put the gloom and doom out of his head—he had to. He only had tonight, and he didn't want to let his worry about the morning get to him.

"Ethan and I will be leaving really early," Justin said to Shirley, "so I wanted to thank you for everything." When she stood, Justin hugged her tightly. "I had no idea what I was walking into when I got here, and I expected to be in and out. But you helped make this visit special."

"Sweetheart, I'm sorry for everything you went through, but I'm glad you were here." She took Justin's hands. "You're always welcome, anytime."

"And you have to come visit me in LA."

Justin hugged her again and then backed away, wiping his eyes. Without saying anything more, Justin took George's hand and with a single look told him exactly what he was thinking. His half-lidded eyes and his tongue peeking over his lips filled in the details. Shirley said good night and hugged Ethan before walking to her living area. George handed Ethan the remote, and they said good night.

Justin led him down the hall to his own bedroom and closed the door. "I didn't realize how hard this was going to be." He stroked

George's cheek and trailed his thumb over his lips. "It isn't supposed to be this hard. We've only seen each other again for a week...."

"But it seems like more."

"I think that's because it is more. You were the one who always saw me for who I was. No one else did that. My folks couldn't. Ethan does, but it's not the same." Justin's voice became rough and hard to understand. "I wish more than anything that I could stay here with you."

"You can't. You have a career and people who are counting on you."

"And you do too. It's in your nature to care for and nurture people. It's what first opened my eyes to the way I loved you." Justin's eyes were intense magnets, and George was caught in their pull. "Do you remember?"

George shook his head. He honestly didn't.

"Of course you don't, because to you it was nothing special. But we were fifteen, and you and I had gone to a baseball game at school."

"That?"

"Yes. See, Billy Humphreys was pitching, and the other team hit a line drive right at him, and he couldn't get out of the way. It hit him, and he went down hard and didn't move. People stood around, stunned, and you were out of your seat and across the field before anyone else could get to him. You and the coach reached him at the same time, and I'll never forget you screaming at the coach to get the fuck away when he tried to move him. I swore you were going to hit him."

"The ball had hit him with enough force that I saw his head snap hard to the side," George said.

"Exactly. You knew he couldn't be moved, and you put your shirt under his neck to stabilize it and told the coach to call an ambulance. When he hesitated, you screamed for him to get his fat ass in gear and do as he was told. There were other expletives, but the dipshit finally listened."

"Billy had broken his neck, and if they'd have moved him, he might have died. I'd just taken a bunch of first-aid classes and knew the rules."

"No. You cared enough to put Billy over the pompous-ass baseball coach, and you were willing to take the heat for it. Billy ended up in a neck brace for months, but he came back to school."

"He's married with three kids now," George said.

"Because of you and that huge heart of yours. I knew then that anyone who would put themselves on the line like that was worth loving. We'd been friends for a long time, but in those few moments, it became more. And it never stopped." Justin's eyes were filled with moisture, and he rubbed them, blinking fast.

"And all I remember from that day was you telling everyone to leave me alone because I knew what I was doing. You stood up for me and ran interference. The adults didn't think a kid knew better than them. Thankfully the EMTs got there fast. See, we all end up counting on you at some point."

"But what about you?" Justin asked. "Are you still counting on me?"

"Yes. But in a different way." It was hard to explain. "You have to do what's right for you, and I won't stand in your way. You've got so much talent, and as much as I want you with me, I know that you're meant to be somewhere else." Sometimes life really sucked in a huge way. He felt they were supposed to be together, and yet they both had commitments at completely different ends of the country.

There was no use discussing this further. They had been over it more than once, and nothing was going to change. He had the night with him and that was all. George tugged Justin closer, and he pressed to George, pushing until George's back hit the wall. Justin slowly approached, anticipation running between them like small electric sparks. Justin had barely touched him, and already George was aching for him. Justin prowled forward, slowly licking his lips.

The wall seemed to be the only thing holding George upright. His knees practically knocked together. When Justin pressed his chest to George's and slipped his knee between his legs, George groaned. This was amazing in a way he didn't quite understand. He and Justin had been together almost every night since Justin arrived. They'd touched, tasted, and felt each other from head to toe. George knew each inch of Justin's drool-worthy body, and he still felt as though he was starving. He gasped for air, trying not to starve his lungs. When Justin's lips finally touched his, it was like a nuclear explosion of passion going off in his head. He clutched Justin, his Justin, and held on for dear life.

Justin lifted him off his feet, and George wrapped his legs around Justin's waist, holding on to him twice now, wanting so much more. He forgot about everything outside the room and what was going to happen tomorrow. All that existed was now, like a bubble encasing them, where nothing else mattered. And for the moment it didn't. Justin carried him to the bed, laying him back, the mattress encasing him as Justin pressed him into it.

A sharp knock stilled them both.

"Yes?" George rasped, closing his eyes and willing whoever was on the other side to go away.

"Justin, it's me," Ethan said.

"What?" Justin snapped.

"It's Roy. He says there's a problem."

The bubble burst and the moment was gone. George sighed and released Justin to let him take care of whatever this was. He closed his eyes and heard Justin open the door. "What is it?"

"Roy explained what's going on. Apparently there's some clause in the deal. The film must be started on Sunday, and that means you have to be on set. It has to do with the money from the producers. As you know, this isn't being backed by a studio but is an independent film, and if the money walks, so does the entire project. I already got us on the earliest flight out in the morning. It leaves just before six. There's nothing else we can do at this point."

"So when do we need to leave?"

"Half an hour, if you want to get any sleep before the flight. I went ahead and booked us a room near the airport so you can rest. I'll go and get your things packed." Ethan looked right at him. "I'm sorry about this, George. I really am," he added just above a whisper and then pulled the door closed.

Justin didn't move. George held his breath, trying to process what had just happened. It felt like Justin was being ripped away from him all over again. It was just like seven years earlier. They were supposed to have one more night, a chance to say good-bye, and now that was gone.

"I don't...." Justin's words trailed off to a sigh. "I wasn't expecting this, and I don't know what to say. Half an hour seems like such a stupidly small amount of time now."

George nodded. Seconds before he'd been wound as tight as a drum, and now he was as deflated as an old tire. He'd counted on just a little more time, and now it was gone. "I know. You have to go."

Justin sat on the edge of the bed. "I need to help Ethan, but I need to say a few things to you." He took George's hand, holding it tightly. "I carry you with me wherever I go. I have for the last seven years, and I will when I leave." He leaned closer, and George threw his arms over Justin's shoulders.

"It's so unfair. It seems like you just got here, and now you have to leave. I knew in my heart that this would come and that getting involved was taking a huge chance. What I didn't realize was how much it was going to hurt."

"Georgie...."

"Don't say anything or feel guilty, because there's nothing you can do. You have to go and I have to stay. There isn't any middle ground, and we both knew that. We can be friends, and we'll talk on the phone and things, but we need to go on with our lives. I've held on to you for far too long, and I think you've done the same." George clasped Justin's hand. "Maybe this is for the best."

"I think you're wrong," Justin told him. "We don't get to choose the people who work their way into our hearts. It happens, and sometimes they leave, and other times they take up residence and stay forever. I know you fall into that second category. So you can move on, and I hope you do. You deserve a life filled with love and care. I wish I could be the one to give you that. But we also need someone to come home to at the end of the day, not someone three thousand miles away."

118

George swallowed. "What do I say to that?"

"Nothing, Georgie. There's nothing to say. I love you and I always will. You have my heart, and that's all there is to it."

Justin blinked multiple times, and George did the same, trying to keep the moisture from spilling down his cheeks.

Justin stood and walked to the door. He had to finish packing, and George figured he could see if they needed any help. Ethan seemed to have everything under control and was already carrying suitcases and his computer bag out to the car. George went to Justin's room and found him closing a single suitcase on the bed. "Ethan is sometimes way too efficient."

"I see that."

Justin closed the suitcase, and Ethan hurried back into the room, took the suitcase, and patted Justin on the shoulder before leaving the room.

"I have to go," Justin said softly. "I want to stay here and say good-bye to you for hours. You have to know that I don't want to go. For the past week, I've felt like I had all of my heart back, and now it's going to be in pieces again."

"I know," George admitted. "I love you too, and I think I always will." He moved into Justin's arms and held him tight, squeezing as hard as he dared before releasing him and stepping back. Shirley came up and hugged Justin and then Ethan, then stepped back to stand next to George. George hugged Ethan as well and then stood as still as he could, watching as they left the house. As soon as the door closed, he walked to the front window, watching as Justin got in the passenger side of the car. Once he shut the door, the interior light cut out, removing Justin from view. Ethan started the engine, then pulled out of the drive and turned toward Gettysburg, the taillights disappearing from sight.

"Sweetheart."

"You don't have to say it, Mom. I knew what I was getting into, and now he's gone."

She squeezed his hand. "All I was going to say was that I was going to miss him."

George nodded slowly. "So am I, Mom." There was nothing left to say.

"Do you regret anything?" she asked him in a whisper.

He thought for a split second. "No." He didn't. "I think if I had it to do over, I'd probably make the same choice. I missed him, Mom, and now I will again. Only before I was missing someone I remembered but who didn't really exist any longer. Now I miss the man he's become, and that's going to be harder to get over."

Thankfully, his mother didn't offer any words of advice. She put her arm around his shoulder and gently hugged him. "I hate that you're hurting. As a mother it's hard to watch. We always want our children to be happy and to have everything they really desire."

"Sometimes reality really bites."

"You can say that again." She let go of him and slowly moved away. George pulled the curtains closed and turned off the lights as he left the room. He said good night to his mother once again, waiting for her to go to her rooms before turning out all the lights and heading down to his bedroom. He stopped in the guest room and lay on the bed. But there was nothing of Justin in here. For days he'd slept in George's bed. He sat back up and pulled the door closed before going to his own room.

He undressed and put his clothes in the hamper before climbing into bed. He really didn't expect to be able to sleep. The bed seemed too big, and he was alone once again.

CHAPTER 7

"Cut!" THE director yelled, and Justin relaxed but stayed in place, waiting for instructions. He was already so sick of this movie, but he couldn't let it show, not for a minute, regardless of how he felt about this asshole director or the fact that the film was so boring no one on God's green earth was ever going to see it. All anyone did was talk, talk, talk—scene after scene of nothing but dialogue around the damn kitchen table. There was little movement in the film. He always sat in the same chair. The only things that changed on the set were the food in front of them or the clothes they were wearing. Damn it, he was hungry. Justin pushed that from his head. He had to stay in character.

"Fuck, I'd kill for a cigarette," Joan, his leading lady, said as the crew worked behind the camera.

"I wish the crap on the table was edible," Harvey, the almost-teenager who played his son in the film, added.

"Me too. But as soon as he gets this scene, we'll break for lunch."

"How do you know?" Harvey asked, wishing he wasn't wearing so much makeup to age him on-screen.

"Because otherwise we'll go on a lunch strike," Justin told him, and Harvey smiled. Justin had really hit it off with the young actor. Harv was a jokester, and Justin had helped him pull off some really good ones on a few crew members. They redirected the suspicion onto Joan, who had a reputation of her own.

"Okay, people. Let's do it one more time. You all know what I want, so let's get this done," the director said, and Justin slipped back into character, scolding Harvey for talking and watching as Harvey crossed his arms over his morose teenager chest. "Action."

They did the scene for the eighth time, and finally Adam, their esteemed director, was happy with what he had. Justin stood, stretching his legs after sitting for hours, and slowly walked to the catering tables, where Ethan waited for him. "That was sheer hell."

"It looked it," Ethan said.

"I need a few minutes." Justin made a lean turkey sandwich and took it to his dressing area, where he closed the door and lay down on the sofa. Silence washed over him. What an amazing lack of sound. That was all he wanted. Well, that and the fact that as soon as he closed his eyes, he thought of Georgie. He'd been thinking about him all the time for weeks.

Ethan came in, placing a glass of water on the table. "Are we ever going to be done with that damn table and chairs?" Justin asked him.

"I think you are," Ethan explained. "That was the last scene in the kitchen. So unless Adam needs to reshoot, you're done and get to move on… to the living room."

"Oh God. I'm going to kill Roy for pushing this project."

"It's going to be a good movie."

"It doesn't feel like it. The whole thing is sapping the energy from my soul. I don't want to be here, and I sure as hell don't want to do any of this." He took a bite and then put the sandwich back on the plate. He wasn't hungry.

"Doesn't matter," Ethan told him. "You need to do the best you can. This could be one of those movies that the critics love and talk about for a long time. That's why you're doing it."

"For an award?" Justin didn't think it was worth it.

"No. You need to do this to prove you can. I know it's cerebral, but you need to prove you can play any role and have the chops to do this."

"It isn't the movie," Justin said, sitting up. He reached for the food and finished it.

"I know exactly what it is. You've been quiet, and your energy levels have sucked since we got back. You don't eat enough. Sure, when you're working, you're fine. You give it your all. But when you're not, you act like the world is coming to an end."

A knock sounded on the door. "Ten minutes."

"Thanks," Ethan called. "Finish your lunch and take the time you have." He left the room, and Justin closed his eyes, trying like hell to clear his head. This whole process was overwhelming, and the short shooting schedule meant that he was working a lot of hours with very little rest. He let his mind wander and kept his eyes closed until he could see George laughing. Warmth spread through him, and he was content.

Justin jerked and nearly fell off the sofa. He looked around, blinking. He figured he must have dozed off for a few minutes. He left the dressing room and wandered back to the set. Wardrobe was waiting for him, and he changed his clothes and then sat in the makeup chair for a few minutes so they could adjust his look. Then he joined the others on set. Everyone had their heads in their scripts, and some pages were thrust into Justin's hand.

"There have been a few adjustments to this scene," the director explained and went into what he wanted. Justin read over the lines and listened to what Adam thought he was looking for. Their director was one of those guys who told you exactly what he thought and then expected something else. So they listened, and Justin did his best to put the words through the Adam-translator portion of his brain to figure out what he really wanted. He thought he might have it, and when Adam said "action," he did the scene. "Great," Adam said when they were done. "Let's do it again." Of course, and they did, two more times, before moving on.

They worked through dinner and well into the evening. Finally Adam called an end to the day, and Justin got in the car, letting Ethan drive him home. Ethan cooked a nice dinner for him, and Justin fell into bed so he could be ready to do it all over again.

"DID YOU hear?" Joan asked as she hurried over, a huge smile lighting up the room. "I'm getting married."

"Phillip finally asked?" Justin said. Phillip was one of the supporting actors, and he and Joan had been making eyes at each other all through filming. They had worked together on a previous film, and the sexual tension between them was becoming overwhelming.

"Yes," she exclaimed, and Justin hugged her gently.

"I'm so happy for you." He kissed her lightly on the cheek. "You deserve all kinds of joy."

"Thanks."

She hurried off to spread the happiness, and Justin watched her go. Fucking hell, he was so jealous of her he wanted to scream. Not that he was interested in Phillip. It was her happiness and the fact that she had someone there who really loved her.

They were two weeks deeper into filming, and it was wearing on him. Justin turned, shuffled to his dressing room, and closed the door. He'd been given an hour, and he intended to use it. Ethan put a plate and a glass of juice on the dressing table and left without saying a word. "Thanks," Justin said and lay down. He was bone tired. Not that he'd done anything physical in weeks, but his mind was turning to mush. This film pulled more and more energy from him. He needed a few days' rest, and he was supposed to finally get some starting tomorrow. He wasn't on the filming schedule for two whole days.

Justin lifted his phone to send George a text: *I'm tired, but have a few days off. I think I'll probably sleep the entire time.*

Is it going better?

I think so. We're past some of the hardest scenes so now it's a matter of finishing the movie. Justin groaned. *There is still a month of filming so anything could change. The script has altered so very much, it's hardly recognizable from what I first read.* He sent the message and started another. *How is it going with your patient?*

Ronda is a sweet lady, and I really like her. Justin knew that George didn't talk about his patients much. It was part of his privacy ethic, and he respected that a great deal. *I miss you.*

I miss you too. He held the phone to his chest and waited for it to vibrate. When it did he saw a picture of George smiling at him. Justin thought of doing the same, but he wasn't sure he could muster a smile. He did it anyway and sent the picture. The smiley face grin he got in return put a real smile on his face. Justin sighed and set his phone on his chest, closing his eyes.

He didn't sleep, though he would have liked to. His phone buzzed, and he checked the display before answering it. "Hi, Roy."

124

"I have another offer for you," Roy told him. "It's as big as the last one."

Justin groaned. "Okay."

"Big sci-fi epic story. One of the studios is scheduling it for a big summer release. Huge press, lots of hype. This one is going to be a game changer."

"I need some time off," Justin said. "I have another month on this film, and then I move to the next one. I'm so tired."

"Then I have some good news. The director they wanted backed out, and they're bringing on a new one. Huge name. But filming is being delayed by two weeks. So you should have some time off, and you'll have almost a month after that one ends before you start this one. I'll send the script over, and you can look at it. They're talking seven figures and a percentage."

"Great, Roy," Justin said.

"Aren't you excited? Or at the very least going to give me grief for something?"

"Yes, I'm excited. That's great, and no, I'm not going to give you grief. You're doing a great job, and I don't tell you that enough." Justin kept his eyes closed and wished he could simply fall into oblivion.

"Something is wrong," Roy said. "Talk to me. Do I need to come down there and kick some ass for you?"

Justin chuckled. "No. I'm worn out. The emotions in this film are sucking the life out of me. That's why I need the time. However you got it, thank you."

"Okay. You haven't been yourself in weeks, and I don't think this is all about the film. Are you sleeping? Do you need anything to help?"

"No, Roy." That was the last thing he needed—sleeping pills or some such crap. Once you started down that road, it was a slippery slope. "I have two days away, and what I need is rest and quiet. Unless someone is dying, please leave me alone. Pretend I'm on a cruise ship in the middle of the ocean with no phones, no lights, no motorcars, not a single luxury…."

"Smartass," Roy said. "So what is going on?"

"I'm tired and maybe lonely."

Roy paused. "Do you need some discreet company? I know people who can help with that."

He knew Roy was only trying to make him happy, but it wasn't working. "No, Roy. I don't want a rent boy or anything like that. Though a chance to have sex with something other than my hand would be nice." He knew that would get to Roy, and the sputtering he heard on the other end of the line said it had worked. "I'm lonely." The whole thing with Joan's engagement had only reinforced how much he missed George. He had expected the longing and need for George to diminish over time, but it hadn't. Every text or phone call seemed urgent and only strengthened his hope. But he wasn't willing to give Georgie up, so he held on to him as tightly as he could.

"You need to get over this. Go out and meet some new people. If you like, I'll throw a party at the house. It'll be a chance for you to meet a number of people."

His first instinct was to say no, but he held back. "That would be nice. Maybe during the two weeks after I'm done filming."

"Awesome." Roy sounded happy, and Justin was glad someone was. "I'll send over the script and forward the contract details."

"Thanks, Roy. Keep running interference for me."

"You know I will." Once he ended the call, Justin wanted to go to sleep, but he got up instead and ate his lunch. Maybe some food would give him a little energy. He took the sandwich, veggie sticks, and salad to the sofa and sat back down. "I'd give anything for a steak right now." He was so tired of eating deli food he was ready to chuck it all.

Justin set down what little was left of his sandwich at a knock on the door. "Come in."

The door opened, and Adam strode in. "You look like hell," Adam said as soon as he closed the door.

"Thanks." Justin scanned him. "And you look like a demented teenager who forgot it's no longer 1982." He cocked his eyebrows.

Adam humphed and sat down without invitation. "Your energy levels seem low."

"I'm tired. You know, Adam, I am a person." He was getting more than a little tired of the hugely compressed shooting schedule, as well as numerous retakes for no apparent reason.

"Don't get me wrong, in front of the camera you're gold, but away from it...."

"So you're here because of my welfare," he said with a half smile. Justin had become suspicious of Adam. Whenever he was nice, there was a knife in one hand. "That's very nice of you. The next few days of rest will take care of what ails me."

"That's the issue. One of the takes isn't working out, and we need to reshoot."

"Then do it on Friday," he challenged. "I can't continue this pace for much longer. I need to rest so I can come back and have something to give you on the rest of the film. You promised me two days off and had arranged the shooting schedule to give them to me."

"Well...."

Justin looked Adam in the eyes, square and unwavering. "Then I have only one question for you. Are you or are you not a man of your word?" He held Adam's gaze until the director turned away. "I always thought you were."

Adding the quasi compliment did the trick. "You're right. I'll have everything set up for Friday It's just a small portion of dialogue that didn't come clear."

"Then loop it. I can fix dialogue easily enough with the sound people."

"Sorry, I wasn't clear. You weren't the source of the error. It was a technical issue and not fixable that way. It shouldn't take long."

"Can we do it tonight?" Justin asked. "I really want to help, but I'm about running on empty."

Adam thought for a minute, then said, "If you're agreeable." He slapped his leg. "We should be done with the scene we're filming soon, and that's the last for today. So yeah. Let's do that."

"Thanks, Adam," Justin said and waited for him to leave before he wolfed down his lunch and spent the rest of the time getting ready.

The day went long. Adam finished their scene hours later, and then they stayed to reshoot. By the time Justin got home, it was nearly midnight. Ethan was good enough to drive him, and he fell asleep in the car on the way.

"You really are wiped out."

"Yeah. This film is kicking my ass. Give me action and permission to blow shit up over this heavy emotional drama."

"You can go to bed and sleep as long as you like in the morning. Leave me your phone, and I'll take any calls that come in." Ethan opened the gate and pulled into the drive. The house was lit up like it was the Fourth of July, and Justin wondered what the hell was going on.

"Kevin," Ethan groaned.

"What the hell is he doing here?"

Justin got out, and sure enough, when he wandered around to the pool, half a dozen guys in tiny bathing suits lounged and swam under the lights. They all stood and hurried over when he came in. Justin greeted each of them and shot daggers at Kevin, who had the grace to stand out of the way.

Ethan hurried over to him, and Justin thought he was going to lay Kevin out right there.

"It's a party." Kevin's voice carried across the water.

"Sorry, guys," Ethan said, turning away. "The party's over. Justin is filming and needs his rest so he can be at his best in front of the camera." Ethan ushered them out as politely as he could. He made sure they all left and then circled back on Kevin like a panther. "Give me whatever key you have." He held out his hand. "You are never to be in here again."

"I was only trying to show him a good time. I'd heard he needed a little pick-me-up, and I thought I'd bring by just the thing." Kevin handed the keys to Ethan and walked to where Justin stood. "Don't worry, we were only out by the pool."

"Never come here again, Kevin," Justin said. "That was bad form, and you know it." He was too tired for all this crap. Kevin left, and Justin sank into one of the lounges, letting the warm night air wash over him. He needed quiet and some peace for just a little while.

"I'll have the locks changed tomorrow," Ethan said.

"I'm sorry I dated him for as long as I did. Who knew that sex twice could exact such a cost?" He didn't even open his eyes. "And he was a dead fish in bed." Justin smiled briefly, then let it fall from his lips. "And at the time I was innocent enough not to know all the things he was into."

"Well, they're gone, and you can go on to bed if you like. I'll set the alarm behind you."

Justin didn't feel like moving, and after a few minutes, Ethan sat down next to him.

"What's going on?"

"Nothing. Roy said he was going to send you some things. A script, some contract details, and he talked about a party during my break once this film is done."

"I saw them and forwarded the files you'll want to your tablet. You can read them when you get a chance. I added the break to your schedule and was wondering if you wanted to go somewhere during the two weeks you have off."

"God, no. I think I'll sleep through most of them." He paused. "On second thought, book us into a resort in Palm Springs for a few days. High end, quiet, with a spa so I can be pampered no end. I want good food, and maybe while I'm there I'll start looking around." He turned to Ethan. "Things would be so much easier if I'd just fallen in love with you."

Ethan smacked his arm and then sat up. "I love you like a brother, but I will never be your second choice for anything. I saw the way you looked at George. For almost a week, he was the center of your universe. When we first met, I used to hope you'd look at me like that, but our relationship went in a different direction, and I'm happy it did. Now that I've seen you in love, really in love, I've decided that's what I want."

"Then we'll both go to Palm Springs and see if we can both get lucky." Ethan deserved to be happy as much as he did.

"Do you really want to get lucky?" Ethan asked.

"I heard what you said, and I think it's time I try to move on." He wasn't sure how successful he'd be, but he had to try.

"I don't think it's going to work."

"We were together only a few days," Justin said, trying to sound practical.

"Yeah," Ethan agreed, "but the heart wants what the heart wants, and it takes time to get over things like this. I'll make reservations at a great place, and we'll have a good time. And if something happens, then it happens, but mostly we'll let you get some rest."

"Hmmm," Justin said, watching the city lights play on the sky. After a few minutes of quiet, his eyes drifted closed. Before he went to sleep, he forced himself to stand up. The lights of the city sparkled in the valley below, and he took a few seconds to admire the glittering carpet that spread out as far as he could see.

"Go on to bed," Ethan told him gently.

Justin went inside and up the stairs to his bedroom. He got undressed and cleaned up before climbing between the soft sheets. It felt good to be home. But as tired as he was, he tossed and turned for an hour, his mind refusing to settle. Eventually he pulled out his phone and called up the pictures he'd taken of Georgie. Scanning through them, he smiled, wishing Georgie were here with him. Eventually he set his phone on the table beside the bed. There was no use wishing. It wasn't going to do him any good anyway.

"THAT'S A wrap!" Adam pronounced a month later. Everyone clapped, and Justin congratulated his costars. Then Adam approached and thanked each of them for their hard work. Ethan had already gathered his things from the dressing room, and Justin was ready to go.

Roy had come on the set to celebrate with him and joined Justin and Ethan in the dressing room. "I'm having a party to celebrate the completion of filming at my house tomorrow night. I'll expect both of you at about eight."

Justin was about to protest, but he'd agreed to the party, and he wasn't going to disappoint Roy and back out. "We'll be there," Justin said.

He was feeling so much better now that the film was actually finished. "But can we please keep the business talk to a minimum?"

"There are a lot of people who want to meet you. Schmooze and talk to people. Make them like you and they'll want to hire you. I promise you a fun time."

"Okay, we'll see you then." He was ready to go home for a huge dinner, but he and Ethan ended up at a restaurant instead. To be truthful, when Justin was working as hard as he had been, he forgot that Ethan worked just as hard to take care of him, so asking him to cook wasn't fair.

"This is really nice," Justin said as they pulled up.

"Joan's assistant, Marty, has been talking about this restaurant for days, so I called. They said they were full, so I dropped your name and they found us a table." Ethan snickered. "This is LA, after all."

They went inside, and Justin wasn't so sure. The place was crowded, and it seemed every head in the place turned to him all at once. The conversations dimmed, and then he heard his name being whispered all over.

"Right this way," the hostess said. "We have a small room in the back, and I reserved that for you." She winked at him. "That will give you some privacy with your boyfriend."

Justin smiled at her. "Ethan is my friend," he said. "I'm not seeing anyone right now."

"Well, that explains it," she said and then blushed strongly. "Please excuse me," she stammered and made sure they were seated before hurrying out of the room.

Justin sat down and then leaned over the table. "You need to find out what she meant."

"Excuse me?" Ethan said.

"Something is going on. I can feel it up my spine," Justin said.

The server approached and thankfully was very professional. He explained the menu and took their drink orders. Once he stepped away, Ethan stood and left the room. Justin sat alone, nervously waiting for Ethan to return.

When he did, he was both pale and shooting daggers. He handed the phone he was on to Justin. "It's Roy."

Justin took it. "What's going on?"

"Did you throw some wild party that you need to tell me about?" Roy demanded in that "I know best" tone he had that was guaranteed to raise Justin's hackles.

"Of course not. I've been too busy to think, let alone do anything but fall into bed for months."

"One of the tabloids got pictures at your house of a bunch of rent boys at a party, and according to the story, at the time the pictures were taken, you were inside with another of the boys. Taking turns."

"I'm going to kill him," Justin said. "Kevin." He saw red. "When we came back from filming one night, Kevin and some of his friends were out by the pool. It turned out he still had access to the house. When we got home, we kicked them all out. I'm not actually in any of the pictures, am I?"

Paper rustled in the background. "No, but it's clearly your house."

"Then call legitimate news outlets and offer them an interview if you like. But for God's sake, don't fill the next two weeks. I need a chance to rest." He could see his quiet time growing wings and flying away.

"I'll see if I can get you a television appearance. This whole thing will blow over quickly. It's the pictures that are important, and they carry no weight without you in them, so relax and we'll let this die down. Meanwhile, chill out and have a good meal. I'll be in touch once I have something."

Roy disconnected, and Justin handed the phone back to Ethan.

"What did he say?" Ethan asked.

"That it was bogus. I wasn't in any of the pictures, so it was pretty lame." Justin calmed down. "But of course he's using it as a chance for me to do some interviews and make television appearances."

"Just make sure it isn't for when we're in Palm Springs. You need a chance to get away, and I have us booked for four days. They promised that they have you in a private suite with secured access. It comes with a therapist who specializes in aromatherapy and massage. I looked her up, and she's supposed to be amazing."

"She…?" Justin asked.

"Yup. No tabloid questions there." Ethan chuckled. "Two can play that game. Everyone knows you're gay, so there won't be any question."

The server returned, and Justin did his best to try to relax and just have a good dinner, but he was as wound up as he could remember being. His head ached a little, but the room they were in was quiet enough that it subsided, and by the end of the meal he was calm once again. But the undercurrent of tension still remained throughout the meal.

"You didn't eat very much," Ethan commented as he drove them home. "I thought you were hungry."

"I'm okay," Justin said. His appetite had flown out the window, which was fine. He didn't need dessert anyway. "I just want to rest."

"I know."

Ethan sped up, and Justin let his mind wander until Ethan pulled into the drive.

Justin went into the house, changed into his suit, and went for a swim. The water was warm, and it leached the tension from his body. He floated in the water, staring at the sky. Sometimes he wished he could see the stars. The lights of the city blocked out all but the brightest ones. Still, it was quiet and subdued, with only the soft glow from the pool lights. He felt more than heard Ethan get into the water. Justin didn't shift. He just let him swim while he continued floating. There was something about being weightless and completely still on a cushion of water that settled his worries and kept his mind from running.

He heard the chime of a phone, but he didn't move as Ethan got out of the water. Justin heard him speaking softly and then the fateful words: "I'll tell him."

"What is it?" Justin asked as he straightened up and put his feet on the bottom of the pool. The tension he'd managed to tamp down came rushing back.

"Just Roy. It seems the man never sleeps. He said he's already set up two television appearances, including one with Jimmy Kimmel.

He said he's also going to get you on *The View* for a little daytime action." Ethan grinned.

Justin wanted to sink under the water. "Fine. I hope you told him about the trip."

"I did."

"Good." He got out of the pool and wrapped up in the robe that Ethan had brought down for him. "I thought that once filming was over, I'd have some time for myself." He shook his head. "I should have known that Kevin was up to something when he just showed up like that. He wanted some attention from someone."

"There's nothing we can do about it now." Ethan was trying to be soothing, but it wasn't working.

"If I get my hands on him, I'm going to wring his neck."

"I have a better idea," Ethan said and picked up his phone. "You don't want to hear any of this."

"Then I'm going to bed," Justin said and went to his room. He stripped off his suit, brushed his teeth, and did his evening regimen before climbing into bed. At one point he felt Ethan come into his room, but he left quickly, and Justin never heard a thing until nearly noon the following day.

God, he felt better after a sound sleep. "Ethan," he called once he was dressed, wandering out to the kitchen. The house was quiet. His phone was on the counter. He picked it up and texted George. He did that every morning, and it was becoming a wonderful habit. He looked forward to his responses. This time he didn't receive one. He dialed his number, but the call went to voice mail. Justin left a message, hoping George was all right. He knew he might have been working and couldn't answer, so he tried to remain calm.

"You're up," Ethan said when he came inside, carrying bags from the grocery.

"What's got you so happy?" Justin said.

"Payback is a bitch," Ethan said as he set the groceries on the counter. "I made a phone call to a friend. Remember last year when you were being stalked?"

Justin shivered. He wasn't likely to forget.

"I still had the number of the police officer who helped us, and I gave him a call last night. It seems Kevin had been on their radar, but only around the edges. I moved him to the middle, and they picked him up at Ambrosia last night. He had plenty of product on him, and right now he most likely is in a cell with a really large new best buddy." Ethan grinned. "That will teach the bastard to mess with my friends." Ethan put away the groceries and then heated up something for lunch.

"What do we have to do today?" Justin asked as he sat on one of the stools.

"You have a party to go to tonight. So I thought we better decide what you wanted to wear or else we'll have to go shopping."

He yawned. "I know what I'm going to wear, so that's no problem. I was thinking we need to get something for you."

"Me?"

"Yeah. I'm tired of you dressing like you're part of the furniture. You take care of me all the time. Finding George again has made me realize that you need to find someone too. So we're going shopping for you for tonight, and you're going to knock them dead."

Ethan paused after opening the microwave. "You do realize that George is on the other side of the country, and that you don't really have him."

Justin sighed. "I can't get him out of my head, Ethan. I know I have to, but I can't seem to do it. I dreamed about him all night long. I have for days."

"Is that why you've had so little energy?"

"I don't know." He wanted to think that he hadn't let the fact that he was missing George to the depths of his soul show to others, but it must have. It was hard filming and wishing that George could see him work, or hearing something funny and the first thing he wanted to do was share it with George. "Last night, with this whole tabloid thing, I wanted to call George right away to make sure he knew it was a lie. All I kept thinking was, what if he sees it? I texted him this morning, and he isn't answering." He hadn't thought about the story in the tabloids when he texted, but the connection hit him as he was speaking.

"He could be at work," Ethan offered.

"Yes. But he usually texts back to say if he's busy." Justin checked his phone one more time and set it back on the counter.

"I know you love him...."

"I do, and it hasn't faded or lessened at all. I want to see him again. Hell, when I suggested Palm Springs, I almost asked about flying back to see him. But that's only going to mean a visit and another good-bye when I have to leave." He wasn't sure he could take that again.

"Everything will be fine." Ethan set a cup of coffee and a small plate of pasta and ham in front of him.

"I'm not so sure." Justin lowered his gaze.

"Time will take care of it. You can't expect your feelings to change in a short time. Do your best not to mope about it." Ethan got a mug of coffee for himself and sat across from him. "You need to eat. You've been doing your best imitation of a bird, and it needs to stop. You're going to get sick, and that isn't going to do anyone any good."

"Has Roy called?" Justin asked before he started eating.

"Yes. He's got you set to make the rounds of the shows. It seems you're a guest in demand. He wanted you to fly to New York...."

"No. I'll call and tell him. If I make that kind of trip, then I'll want to stop in Pennsylvania, and that's going to take more time." There was no way he was going to go that far and not try to see George.

"I know how you feel, but if you get a really great opportunity in New York, you can't turn it down. And you'll be on a plane, fly in, do your interview, and then fly home because you'll have another interview a few days later. It's the business you're in, and you know it."

Justin growled, even though he knew Ethan was right.

"Let me call Roy so I can work out the details of your schedule," Ethan said, and Justin backed down. He continued eating while Ethan made his call. "No, Roy. He is not doing that," he heard Ethan say from the living room. "Would you want that kind of schedule? And don't you dare try to bullshit me in order to get what you really wanted in the first place. He's taking four days off starting tomorrow afternoon. We'll be out of town." It grew quiet, and Justin knew the two of them were working. "Fine, he can live with that." Another silence. "Eat shit, you asshole," Ethan said without heat and came back into the room. "Here's your schedule for the next two weeks. I told Roy he was not to book anything else. You do need to fly to New York, but you'll be there two days and do three interviews and shows. That's after we get back from Palm Springs. Then you have some interviews and appearances here in town the week before you film, but you should be good. I went ahead and told him to make travel arrangements, and he's booking you in the Plaza in New York."

"I've always wanted to stay there," Justin said.

"He said that part is his gift for doing all this."

"A gift from Roy." Justin put his hand over his heart and acted like he was going to swoon. "What's gotten into him?"

"I don't know. I think he was feeling bad for cutting into your off time, but he says with so many films in production and getting ready for release, you need to be a hot property. And of course he's right. This will be good."

"I know, but I don't want to spend all my time working."

"You won't. I'll see to that."

Justin looked over the schedule and saw how they'd grouped the interviews together so he'd have quiet days to himself. "Maybe we can have a few friends over one evening. Not a blowout party, but something quiet. It would be nice to reconnect with people."

"I can help with that. See—here." He pointed to the schedule. "Just tell me who to invite, and I can take it from there."

"You're way too good to me," Justin said.

"I think we're good to each other."

Justin put both hands on the counter. "Let's go. We need to get you something to wear before tonight."

He drove the Ferrari to Melrose.

THAT EVENING, the traffic to get to Roy's was crazy. He must have invited half of Hollywood. As they got close to the house, a valet approached him, and Justin gave him the keys to the car and left the parking to someone else. By the time he arrived at the house, his car was parked right out front. He and Ethan entered the fray, and Roy's wife, Charlotte, greeted both of them cheerfully. Sometimes Roy did the Hollywood thing in an over-the-top way, but Charlotte was always warm and genuine.

"I'm glad you're here," she said, hugging both of them. "The boys are out by the pool talking business. Roy asked me to send you out when you got here." Her smile dimmed. "I told him if he talked business all night, I was going to push him into the pool."

"I knew I liked you," Justin told her. "And I promise if he tries to talk too much business, *I'll* push him in. He promised me fun and some relaxation."

"I think he has the fun part covered," Charlotte said with a glint in her eyes. "Go on through," she said as she motioned and took Ethan's arm. There weren't as many people as Justin feared. All the cars must be there because someone else was having a party.

"Justin," Adam said as he entered the living room. "It's good to see you." He seemed genuinely happy. "The scenes we got were amazing, and we're going to have a powerful film."

"I'm surprised you aren't in the editing room," Justin said.

"I was there all day, and we made some tough decisions. Now the editors are doing their thing, and we'll pick up again in a few days. It's going to be awesome, and you are the focal point of almost every scene you were in."

"I'm glad you're pleased. It was a tough shoot because of the material, and you pulled so much out of me. I learned a great deal from you."

"I did the same. You did the best when I let you do what comes naturally."

Adam introduced Justin around, and he shook hands with the men Adam was with, talking with them briefly.

"I'll be seeing you in a few weeks," Justin said to Dominic Keller, a well-known director.

"Yes, you will, and I'm looking forward to it. If everything Adam says is true, we're going to have an awesome experience,"

Dominic said with a genuine smile. "I think someone is trying to get your attention out by the pool."

"It seems so," Justin said before excusing himself. He walked out to the pool, where Roy was staring at him.

"I was wondering when you were going to get out here," Roy said, and Justin wondered what the hurry was. He always made sure to say hello to everyone. "I think you know everyone," Roy said, and Justin wondered if he'd lost his mind. Of course he knew all the people Roy was talking to. It was Ethan, Roy, and Charlotte. Roy stepped aside, and George stood between him and Charlotte.

Justin blinked, unable to believe his eyes. George moved closer, and it wasn't until Justin felt George's arms around him and had his rich scent fill his nose that he allowed himself to believe this was real. Up until then he thought it had to have been his imagination playing awful tricks on him.

CHAPTER 8

"HOW DID you get here?" Justin asked first, hugging George tighter. "Why are you here? Don't think I don't want you here, because I do, but my God, I can't believe this."

"Justin, relax, take a breath. I'm not going to disappear in a puff of smoke," George whispered as Justin buried his head in his neck and showed no sign of letting him go. "There are people all around us."

"So? At this moment, you're the only one who matters."

Justin made no move to release him, and George closed his eyes and let contentment replace the stress and worry of cross-country travel. Eventually Justin stepped back. Then he looked to Roy and Charlotte as well as Ethan, who were all grinning like Cheshire cats.

"These lovely people flew us out for a while."

"Us? Is Shirley here?" Justin asked, looking around.

"George's mother is in town too, and my mother is showing her around," Charlotte said. "They went out to dinner and to do some shopping. Though they'll be back in an hour or so."

"How long can you stay? What are your plans? Ethan and I were going to Palm Springs tomorrow. Is there…?"

Justin was hyped up big-time, and it thrilled George that he was so excited.

"Justin, you and George are going to Palm Springs," Ethan told him. "If you'd looked closely enough at that reservation, you'd have seen it's for two with a king bed. I was hoping you'd be too busy to notice."

"But what about you?" Justin asked Ethan.

"I'm going to stay here and have a few days of peace and quiet without you." Ethan grinned. "I'll go out and see how much trouble I can get into. You two go and have fun."

Justin took George's hand and held it tightly. He thanked all of his friends for the surprise and then excused himself and tugged George with him. The next few hours were a whirlwind for George. He met tons of people, names he'd heard or seen on movie screens— important people who talked and listened to Justin like an equal. George supposed he was. But they also asked about him, and when he told them about the small town he lived in, they peppered him with questions. It seemed all of them had films coming up set in quirky places, and they wanted some background.

"Is there really a town gossip?" one man asked.

"No, there are dozens," George answered, still holding Justin's hand like it was an anchor in case this turned out to be a dream. It sure as hell felt like it, and whenever he turned to Justin, the light shining in his eyes was breathtaking.

"Adam," Justin called, and a young man with dark, wavy hair approached. "I'd like you to meet George." They shook hands. "Adam and I just wrapped up filming."

"It's good to meet you, George," Adam said, his eyes bouncing between them. "I see…."

"What?" Justin asked.

"Remember I told you I was worried about your energy? You seemed tired. I think we found the cure."

Adam's expression wasn't one George could read.

"Don't get me wrong. His work was stunning, but we were worried about him. I see now it was loneliness. He was missing you."

"Adam…."

"It's a good thing, Justin. We…." He turned to the other directors he'd been talking with. "All of us get wound up in our projects. They become like our children, and it requires stamina and hard work, long hours. But we all have something in common—a partner who's at home willing to stand behind us even when we're complete bastards. You need that too."

Justin shot Adam a mischievous grin, and George braced himself for what was to come.

"You had that part down a few times."

The respect between the two of them was clearly evident.

Adam nodded, so George could see he didn't take offense. Adam and Justin had a relationship, and a stab of jealousy raced through him. George knew there was nothing romantic between them, but Adam knew Justin in a way that George never would. Justin moved closer to him, putting his arm around George's waist.

"Sure I did. It's what it takes to get the job done, and you all stepped up and made it happen. That cast was a dream team."

"Was it good to push him like that?" George asked once Adam had been called away.

"He and I are at the 'we've been through hell and come out the other side' stage, so it's okay. Adam is an amazing director. But it's something you don't see when you're in the middle of things. It's only once the work is over and you can see the whole picture that you realize just how incredible he was, and by then it's over."

George followed Justin throughout the house and yard, meeting people, listening as Justin engaged everyone and made sure he was included in all the conversations. Everyone here was far out of his league, and George knew he should be intimidated, but Justin made it seem normal and like he belonged. "Remember, they all put their pants on just like you," Justin whispered to him at one point. "And out of their fancy clothes and cars they don't look anywhere near as amazing as you."

"Justin," George said, heat rising to his cheeks.

"It's true. There's something to be said for being real, honest, and who you are."

Justin continued circulating. Servers made their way through the gathered partygoers, and George nibbled the bites and then excused himself, planning to bring Justin something from the bar and get a drink for himself.

"Do you think you're going to like it here?" one of the bartenders asked as he made the drinks. "I saw you with Mr. Hawthorne and heard others talking about how you just arrived."

"I'm just here for a visit," he answered. But the truth was that George wasn't sure how he was going to be able to go home again. It had torn him apart when Justin had returned to LA, and when Ethan had contacted him, offering to fly him and his mother out to see Justin during his break in filming, George had initially been resistant. He hadn't been sure it was a good idea, but the idea of spending time with Justin again was more than he could pass up.

"It looked to me like you're close." The bartender handed George the drinks. "I hope everything works out for you." The bartender smiled and turned to the next person, and George carried the drinks to where Justin was standing by the side of the pool, waiting for him.

The heat in his eyes was searing, and George wondered if everyone saw the intensity in Justin's expression. He kept his attention glued to him, and the heat only grew in intensity as George approached.

"I was wondering where you went," Justin said.

"I thought you could use something after all the talking you've done." He handed Justin a glass of soda with lime and sipped his martini. "The party is nice."

"Yes, it is," Justin agreed without turning away. "Did your mother arrive?"

"About an hour ago. Ethan is showing her around, and apparently Mother is charming everyone." George turned to where his mom was talking with a group of agents and directors. She was telling some story, and they all looked enthralled. "I think she's having a great time."

"That's good." Justin didn't look away.

"What's gotten into you?" George asked.

"Nothing. Right at this moment I'm enjoying the best view in the entire city." Justin set his glass on one of the tables without looking away. "I missed you. Every night you were in my dreams."

"Mine too," George confessed. "The bed seemed too big and the house too empty. Mother kept cooking like she was trying to feed an army. I think she fell back into the habit of feeding our family, and now a lot of the time it's just her because of the hours I work." George finished his drink and set his glass next to Justin's. "You sound as though you've been busy."

"I have, and every minute I wasn't on set or when it was quiet, I had this urge to call you and tell you what was happening."

"Justin," Roy said, clapping him on the shoulder. "Why don't you say your good-byes? We'll make sure Ethan and Shirley get home."

"Roy...."

"Just go," he said with a smile. "Spend some time with George."

"Thanks," Justin said and took George's hand, leading him to where his mother and Ethan stood with yet another group of people.

"Are you having fun?" George asked.

"Sweetheart, this is an amazing party." She greeted Justin with a kiss on the cheek.

"George and I are going back to the house," Justin told Ethan. "Roy said he's arranged for you to go when you're ready."

"We're fine. Go ahead," Ethan said, and Justin hustled George out of there quickly, probably before anyone else could get his attention. Justin was in such a hurry, and he was laughing the entire time as they made their way out to the car.

George stopped, looking at Justin as though he'd lost his mind when he opened the door of the Ferrari. "Your chariot awaits."

"Cheesy," George said, sliding into the seat as Justin got in and started the engine. Its purr turned to a roar as he backed out of the drive and zoomed down the steep hillside road.

"I love the feel of this car," Justin called out over the wind as he took the corner like the car was glued to the road. It was amazing.

"It's awesome." George could get used to this. "Are we taking this to Palm Springs?" He was so looking forward to a few days alone with Justin.

"We can, sweetheart. Whatever makes you happy." Justin sped up and slipped onto the freeway for a mile or two. Then he got off and they zipped along city streets until they started climbing once again. Justin's house was just what George expected: modern but comfortable. As the gate closed behind them, Justin pulled right into the garage and waited for him to get out of the car.

"I guess Ethan is bringing our luggage over with him," George said. "He said to pack light."

Justin kicked the door closed behind him and pressed George against it, kissing away his words and any thought other than him. George shook in Justin's arms. He'd wanted this for weeks, months, and now it was here. Justin pressed to him, kissing him, holding him.

"Bedroom?" George asked during a break for breath.

"Fuck no!"

Justin pulled George's shirt over his head and then kicked off his shoes and socks. By the time George could do the same, Justin had stripped him naked, and he stepped out of his pants. Justin took him by the hand, leading him through the house, and pulled open the doors to the pool. The sun had set, and as the lights came on, George turned and stepped down into the water, diving under and letting the warmth cradle him.

When he surfaced he looked for Justin and found him as he stepped out of his pants, a tanned, toned vision walking toward him, his cock pointing the way. George's mouth watered at the lean power on display. He followed him with his eyes, every graceful movement a study in fluidity as Justin stepped into the pool and slowly descended into the water, hiding the deliciousness from view. It hardly mattered, though. Justin was next to him, gently tugging him away from the side of the pool and into his strong arms.

Justin guided George's lips to his, and he wrapped his legs around Justin's waist, letting the water and Justin support him. Justin cupped his ass, holding him firmly as he kissed George to within an inch of his life.

"I can't believe you're here."

George felt cradled in Justin's arms, like nothing could happen to him while he had them around him.

"Ethan made all the arrangements a week or so ago. He said you'd been pushing yourself and hadn't been eating well. That, of course, pushed all of Mom's buttons, and she couldn't get out here fast enough so she could try to fatten you up." George looked down between them. "Though you look plenty healthy to me."

He wriggled his hips, and Justin groaned as his cock slid along George's crack.

"Ethan's a mother hen."

"He cares about you a lot and is intent on taking care of you."

"But didn't you have to work?" Justin asked.

"Things haven't been the easiest back home. My last job was only for a few weeks, and then my patient passed away in her sleep. It was peaceful, but the care is expensive, and a lot of people can't afford it. So when I get back, I'm going to apply to every hospital I think I can drive to and hope for the best. I liked helping people in their homes, but it isn't working out right now. I'd been working very steadily, but now it's like people don't need me." George tried to keep his disheartened feelings out of his voice.

"I need you," Justin said. "I've spent three months and the filming of an entire movie with all the drama and intensity that entails trying to get over you, and nothing works. I spent a week getting to know you again, and I know I'll never get you out of my soul."

"But we're right back where we were," George said.

"Maybe. The difference is that you're here now. I have two weeks to convince you that you can't live without me."

Justin cut off George's attempted arguments with a searing kiss that sent heat through him so strongly he was surprised the water didn't steam. As they kissed, the water swirled around them as Justin slowly propelled them toward a shallower spot.

"I want you," Justin groaned, and George whined softly under his breath as Justin teased his opening. "I need to feel this is you and not some dream, and I need to know that you're still mine."

"God, you sure know how to sweep a guy off his feet… literally," George said as Justin sat him on one of the steps and rose out of the pool like a Roman god emerging from the sea.

"Stay right there," Justin said and turned away, walking naked into the house. He returned a minute later with a stack of towels that he set next to the pool. Without a word, Justin descended into the water once again and lifted George into his arms. "You get more stunning every time I see you."

"Now that's a lie," George said.

"No, it isn't. You are breathtaking," Justin said, lifting him up until he floated on top of the water, Justin supporting his hips and butt. The air had a nip to it, which teased his exposed skin, making his cock jump in anticipation. "I see part of you is more than a little excited."

"Fuck that *little* shit," George said.

Justin grinned at him. "How about if I do this instead?"

Justin winked and leaned forward, sucking him deeply into his mouth. George had to stop the urge to flail, and he lay still even as Justin did wicked things to him with that talented mouth and tongue of his. He bobbed his head, the heat from his mouth alternating with the cooler water, making George as erotically unsettled as he could possibly remember.

"You're evil," George muttered.

"Should I stop?" Justin asked, doing just that.

"Don't you fucking dare," George cried, and Justin took him once again.

George shook and quivered, trying to flex his hips, but of course that did nothing because while he balanced on Justin's hands, the rest of him was on water and he could get no purchase at all. Justin knew he was at his mercy, and he was obviously loving George's increased frustration.

Finally Justin let his hips sink under the water. George managed to get his feet on the bottom, but his head was still floating on a cloud. Justin guided him to the side of the pool and up onto a flat lounge that he covered with towels. George flopped onto his belly, and Justin stroked his feet and up his calves and thighs. "What are you…?" Justin's magic fingers continued their slow upward movement, caressing his cheeks and sliding deliciously down between them before continuing their wanderings.

"I'm going to show you how much I've missed you."

Justin's hot breath tingled against his wet skin, and when Justin parted his cheeks, George gasped and gripped the edge of the lounge. He felt Justin press his face between his cheeks, and he mewled like a wild cat at the head-spinning sensation that barreled through him.

"Justin…," George moaned softly, his feet pointing and his legs throbbing as he did his best to part them.

"Sweetheart, you hang on, because I'm going to give you the ride of your life."

And damn if Justin didn't do just that. And when George thought things couldn't get any hotter, Justin climbed on the lounge, draping his heat over him, cock nestled right into his crease, arms around his chest, clutching them together.

Justin only released him long enough to slip on the condom, and then he was right back. George was surrounded by Justin on the outside while Justin slowly slid inside. It was heady.

"I didn't think I'd feel like this ever again."

"I'm beginning to think that you and I are fated." Justin pressed fully inside him and held still.

"God, I hope so," George groaned.

"It's the only explanation." Justin slowly began to move. "We were too young when we first met, and I think we were a little stupid this last time."

They rocked together slowly, with Justin sending him to heaven. There was a fleeting conscious thought about hoping like hell his mother and Ethan didn't come home, because he did not want his mother to see him like this. But then Justin changed angles, and he didn't fucking care if the Google satellite was overhead taking pictures of them for the world to see.

"How about the fact that I love you," George moaned, throwing his head back.

Justin slid his hand gently around George's neck, cradling his throat and sucking on his ear. George closed his eyes, letting Justin take over. It was too much to take in, and he had to shut off one of his senses so the others could heighten.

"I love you too, and I've missed you each and every day." Justin vibrated the chair with each thrust, sending ripples through George's body.

"I'm going to come," George whimpered, losing control. He kept his eyes clamped shut, letting the sensation overtake him. He cried out, sending his rapturous release into the night with Justin following behind.

Neither of them moved, staying still as though the spell between them would break at any moment. Not that George didn't understand. Things between him and Justin had a tendency to break and pull them apart.

"Justin?" he whispered after a few minutes.

"Yes, Georgie?"

"I think we need to move."

"Maybe."

Justin wriggled teasingly and then withdrew from his body and stood, helping George up. Justin wrapped him in one of the large towels and guided him back onto the lounge.

"But I think you and I have to talk."

George nodded slowly. The entire flight out here, he knew this was coming. Yes, he and Justin had spent a week together, and he and his mother had been invited out, but little about their circumstances had changed. He was expecting Justin to say that this was the end. They needed to go on with their lives; George knew that. It would be hard to hear but practical. Justin needed a chance to love and be loved, and so did he. "I think you're right."

"We've been deluding ourselves," Justin said.

"I agree. We have." He hated to admit it, but it was true.

Justin leaned forward. "No, I don't think you're understanding me. But I'll do what you want."

George shook his head. This was confusing, and it was getting them nowhere. "Wait. Let's talk openly instead of trying to second-guess what we're trying to say. I understand that you can't live in Pennsylvania. Your life and work are here, and you'd be traveling all the time even if you did move there, so that's no use. I still need to help take care of my mother, and our lives are there. She's doing well now, but it won't always be that way." He pushed away that train of thought. "What are you proposing?"

Justin stood and extended his hand. George took it, and Justin tugged him to his feet and led him to the edge of the pool, then pointed out.

"That's the pool house. It was originally intended as a guesthouse or a place where a caretaker or property manager could live. It would make a great suite for your mother. It has its own entrance, and she would be able to come and go as she pleased."

"Wait, you're saying you want my mother and me to move out here?" George asked.

"Yes. I thought I could get over you, but I can't. You're part of me, and you have been for a long time. I tried for months to get you out of my head. But when I saw you at the party, I knew I wasn't going to let you just walk away from me. I was going to try to give you a reason to stay. You can get all the work you could possibly want."

George was floored. This was not at all what he'd expected Justin to want to talk about. "You have to be kidding me. You're asking me to give up my life at home and move across the country."

"I'm asking you to come here and build a life with me," Justin said. "I've come to realize that I never should have let you go, especially not twice. I shouldn't have run the first time, and I should have figured out what I really wanted months ago and had the guts to ask you. Instead I hid behind what was convenient and easy. I think I've done that too much when it comes to the relationships in my life."

"You're serious?" George said, swallowing hard as the possibility of happiness with Justin opened up in front of him like a huge present on Christmas morning. It was almost too good to be true.

"Of course I am. I don't expect you to give me an answer right away. But I'd ask you to think about it and talk to Shirley."

"Justin."

He turned as Ethan came outside. George's cheeks heated as Ethan stepped around the clothes they'd left around the pool deck and hurried over.

"I saw this at a newsstand on the way home."

Ethan pressed the flimsy tabloid magazine into Justin's hand. Justin went pale almost immediately, and his hand shook.

"Oh my God." Justin swallowed, and George caught him before he went down onto the concrete. "Did you read the article?"

"Yeah. It gives no details, but says that when you left Pennsylvania to come to Hollywood, something terrible happened to cause it. They speculate that you did something bad, but they don't give any details."

"Can they just write whatever they want?" George asked.

"Pretty much. But this hits so close to home. I mean, according to these rags, I've fathered half a dozen children before I figured out I was gay and had orgies by the score at this house." Justin gasped for air.

George knew exactly what this was doing to him. "Let's get you in the house," he said, helping Justin up.

"I need to call Roy," Ethan said.

"No. Justin is more important."

George got Justin on his feet and guided him into the house. Somehow he managed to do it without flashing his ass at Ethan or his mother, who was waiting inside. Ethan fussed and guided them down through the large house to Justin's huge master bedroom.

"I'm okay," Justin said, but George didn't move away until Justin was safely sitting on the edge of his bed. "I should be used to these things always feeling like a sneak attack."

George hurried away and returned with a glass of water that he pushed into Justin's hand. "How can anyone get used to that?"

"You don't," Ethan answered. "Most of the time the stories are so laughable that you pay no attention and go on. But this one is either the luckiest shot on earth, or someone has been doing some digging since his trip back to Pennsylvania. I suspect they got a few facts and made the rest up."

"George, would you get my clothes for me?" Justin asked.

George left and retrieved their clothes from where they'd left them strewn around the house. Shirley watched him as he piled everything in his arms.

"Don't say anything," he warned her and hurried back to Justin's room. Ethan left them alone to dress and then returned once they were presentable. By then Justin wasn't nearly as pale and seemed to be over the initial shock.

"What do we do?" George asked.

"I have to call Roy," Justin said. "Go on out to the living room and give me a few minutes. I'll join you as soon as I'm done."

George didn't want to go, but Justin seemed firm, so he left with Ethan, taking a seat in the living room next to his mother.

"What can we do to help?" his mother asked.

"We need to be there for him," Ethan said. "He and Roy will come up with a basic plan of attack."

"Is it always like this?" George asked.

"No. Lately Justin has gotten more attention from the tabloids than usual, but that's probably because he's on the rise. This happens."

George heard Justin's footsteps and turned to him as he approached. "What did he say?"

"He'd already seen it and was ready. He said that we've got what we need in place and that I'm to do the shows and interviews as scheduled." Justin sat next to George and leaned on his shoulder. "Until then I'll be damned if I'm going to let them change our plans." Justin looked up from where he sat.

"Good. You two go to the desert and have a good time. I'm going to show Shirley everything there is to see here in LA."

Ethan smiled conspiratorially at Shirley, and George wondered what exactly Ethan and his mother had planned.

"And you and George are going to have the time of your lives while you figure things out between you."

"What?" they said in unison.

Ethan turned to George's mother, who nudged him and nodded. "Shirley and I really hit it off when we were in PA." He smiled at the local reference to the state name. "So when I got the idea to bring George out to visit, I called Shirley, and it seemed we both were sick and tired of the moping. I found out that George has been just as down and miserable as Justin. So when we arranged to bring him out, she decided to come too."

"You knew?"

"That you were staying for me? Of course. A mother knows these kinds of things. And I'll have you know that if I never see snow again, it'll be too soon."

Justin chuckled, and George realized he was being ganged up on in the best way possible.

"Does she know?" George asked, turning to Justin, who shook his head. All this was a little too much for him to take in all at once.

"No decisions need to be made right away, but both of you need to figure out what you want. I think you've been caught in between for so long that some clarity and time are needed. Ethan and I will be fine, so you can go and have a good time." His mother yawned.

Ethan sprang into action. "Come with me, Shirley. I'll show you to your room. I'm putting her in the pool house."

Sometimes Justin wondered if Ethan was a mind reader.

"Then you can get settled, and I'll bring you your luggage." They chatted as he led her out of the room.

"It seems we each have someone pushing us," George said with a chuckle. "I have been morose since you left. It's hard saying good-bye to the other half of your soul."

"Yes, it is," Justin agreed. "Let's get your luggage. You have to be tired, and we have a big day tomorrow."

They found their bags in the hallway. Justin hefted one, and George carried the other, following Justin to his room. He knew he had a very big decision to make, one that would change his entire life. But that would be there in the morning, and hopefully sleep would shed some light.

THE RIDE to Palm Springs was amazingly warm, and riding in the Ferrari was like a dream. He and Justin spent four days in peace. The only phone calls Justin got were his agent, once, and when Ethan called each day, but those calls seemed to be him making sure everything was okay. George and Justin were pampered, massaged, treated, soaked, and relaxed into a completely new state of mind. And after four days, Justin drove back to LA looking like a new man. The tension had been leeched out of both of them.

"We never talked about my offer," Justin said.

"No, we didn't," George agreed. "And I have to say it's tempting, but...." George watched the desertscape pass outside the car. Justin had the top up because of the dust. "I don't want to be dependent on you. I need to pay my own way, and I can't afford anything at your house. I mean, I can't pay room and board or help with anything."

"I don't need help with money. What I do is incredibly draining. I need you to be there for me. And I don't mean to do the laundry, cooking, and cleaning. I have a service for all that. What I want is for you to be my family, and I want to be your family."

"But my mother...."

"She's part of your family... *our* family. That's what I want from you. Nothing more. If you want to work, then do so. I've had people who wanted to live off me my entire career, and I've had to be careful. I know I don't have to do that with you." Justin's phone rang, and he answered it on speaker. "What is it, Ethan?"

"Are you on your way back?" Ethan asked.

"We're an hour or so away, depending on traffic."

"Everything is all set for the morning. A limousine is going to pick us up to take us to the airport at five, and I've already got your bag partially packed. Shirley is making us dinner tonight. She insisted. And then you can get some rest."

"Is there any change to the schedule?"

"No. But one of the mainstream news outlets has picked up on the story from the tabloid. They haven't been nasty, but *Entertainment Tonight* did ask about what happened on the show last night."

"Great," Justin said. "I'll see you when we get home." He hung up. "I had hoped some parts of my life could remain private."

"Just say nothing. Won't they get tired of it once someone else goes into rehab?" George recalled dozens of those stories over the years.

"Maybe. But this raises questions about my integrity and image. Those are all I have in this business. If directors or the studios think

I've been lying to them or hiding things, my career prospects will dry up fast. I like what I do, and I want to be able to keep acting if I can."

"You've never lied to anyone," George said. "Where could all this be coming from?"

"It doesn't have to come from anywhere. Someone wrote a juicy story designed to whet the appetite, and it did. Now it's gaining traction." The tiny lines around Justin's eyes that had disappeared during their visit to the spa were now back.

George sat back because he had nothing more to offer. This wasn't his strength. He could fight off an enemy that he saw coming, but he couldn't fight what seemed to hide in the shadows. "If I could make this go away, I would."

"I know. It's the dark side of the business I'm in. People gossip about nothing."

Justin sped up and grew quiet as he drove the rest of the way to his house. And once they arrived, Justin spent a long time on the phone with his agent, sat down to dinner, and then spent part of the evening on the phone. They'd had four days together, but already Justin seemed to be pulling away once again.

"Is it always like this?" George asked Ethan as they sat outside near the pool. He was tired of being in the house.

"I won't lie to you. Justin is a busy man. When he's filming, he works long days, and when he's home, there's something that requires his attention."

"So what does he need me for?" George asked.

Justin joined them without his phone in hand. He settled in the chair next to George's, and Ethan quietly got up and left. Justin was tense; the air around him crackled.

"I don't want to go. All this was planned before I knew you were coming. But with these stories...." He turned. "I could cancel all of it and stay here with you. It seems a shame to have you come all this way and not spend every second with you." Justin leaned across the space between their chairs. "I was hoping to be able to convince you to stay."

"I know you were, and though we haven't talked about it more, I'm thinking about it. I honestly am." He had little doubt about how Justin felt about him now, but would that change? The life Justin had here was nothing like what George was used to, and he wasn't sure he'd ever fit in or understand it. At the party, he'd been with Justin and people had been nice, but he saw the occasional looks people gave him. Probably wondering where he came from and what he was doing there. They all had their fancy clothes, and he was in the same things he wore back home. He was on the verge of putting his doubts aside, closing his eyes, and making the leap. But he held back. If he made this change and agreed to stay with Justin, then as far as he was concerned it was for life, and he needed to make a very careful decision.

CHAPTER 9

JUSTIN QUIETLY got out of bed and went into his bathroom. The clothes he was going to wear had been set out on the counter so he could dress without waking George. He cleaned up, dressed, and turned out the light. When he entered the bedroom once again, he listened to George's soft breathing and came closer to his side of the bed.

George didn't stir, and Justin watched him sleep. He hated leaving like this. It was only for a few days, but George hadn't given him an answer yet, and Justin was scared shitless that he would decide to go back to Biglerville permanently. He had most definitely been sincere in his offer, but he had thought it best not to push. George wasn't someone to take important decisions lightly, and he needed time to think things over. Justin hoped that in the end, George would decide in their favor.

He knew that George was well aware of how he felt. Justin had been able to make that very clear over the past few days in Palm Springs. Hell, the time had been magical. More than once he'd stared into George's eyes and had been struck breathless at the love he'd seen glowing in them. He leaned over the bed and gently kissed George's cheek.

"Justin," Ethan whispered through the cracked-open door.

Justin turned and left the room, taking one last look at George's sleeping form before closing the door.

"The limousine will be here in five minutes."

"I feel like I'm abandoning them."

"Would I let that happen?" Ethan asked. "Charlotte is coming over later this morning to take them to lunch and show them around. Tomorrow Adam's family is going to take them to Disneyland. He has to work, and his wife called because she knew we had out-of-town guests. She's an amazing lady, and she knows what it's like to be married to someone in the movie business."

157

"Is this more of you and his mother's matchmaking?"

"I have never been a yenta," Ethan said haughtily. "I thought this would be a chance for him to ask questions. The business can be one hell of a bitch for a taskmaster, and you know it."

"I want him to stay," Justin said.

"Under false pretenses? I doubt it." Ethan gave him one of those looks his second-grade teacher used to use. "Don't worry. Eve is a sweet lady. She and I talked a lot while you were working with her husband. You'll love her."

"Adam and Eve?" Justin asked.

"Yes. It's a hoot. She has a real sense of humor about it. She's kinky too. She said she loves to tie her husband to the bed and feed him apples while telling him he's been a bad boy." Ethan rolled his eyes and laughed at his own joke. "Come on. Our ride will be here any minute, and they'll be just fine. Roy tightened up the schedule a little, so you'll be home tomorrow evening and can still have the three interviews you need to do. So let's go."

Ethan opened the door, and the driver came inside to get their bags. They followed him out, and Justin got into the back of the car with Ethan following him inside. The driver closed the door.

They began to move, and instantly Justin hated it. The thought that he was leaving George yet again made him crazy. He pulled out his phone and typed out a text that he sent to George. He didn't want him to think he'd left without telling him good-bye. Justin had already done that once in his life, and it was something he didn't want to ever repeat.

"This is going to be a fast trip, and it's going to be exhausting," Ethan warned.

"What would I do without my mother hen?"

"All I'm saying is that you need to relax and rest on the plane. There should be time to prepare for the interview once we get there. Marcheta is a friend, and you know she's been tabloid fodder, so she's going to help you set the record straight."

"I know. But I have to decide what I'm going to say." Justin had run over and over in his head just how much of his painful past he wanted to reveal. The pain of that part of his life was something he'd told almost no one about, and he wanted to keep it private.

"Just explain about your father kicking you out for being gay. That's safe and will be enough to get people's sympathy. You can say that you were there when your father passed away, and that you were able to make a sort of peace in the end. That should set the record straight. Of course, you also talk about your upcoming films to help promote them."

"I know the drill," Justin said, annoyed at first, but he let it go. Ethan was just doing his job, and he always did it well.

"Yes, you do, but it never hurts to get a pep talk every once in a while. Would you rather have it from me or Roy?" Ethan cocked his eyebrows.

"Okay. I see your point."

"I thought so. Just relax and be yourself. That's what the fans respond to." Ethan finally sat back, and Justin closed his eyes, enjoying some quiet time where he could be alone with his thoughts. When they pulled up to the terminal, he got out and let Ethan handle the luggage. He figured the whole disguise wasn't going to work, not with the limousine and everything, so he waited while Ethan checked in curbside, stepping forward when they needed to check his ID. Then they headed inside to security, where he was sent through a more private screening area and then to the first-class lounge where he could sit quietly and wait for his flight.

Ethan brought him a cup of coffee, and he sipped it while he waited, checking his phone. He'd been hoping for an answer from George, but as it got closer and closer to boarding time, he figured George was still asleep and hadn't seen his message. Their flight was called, but Justin and Ethan held back. They could board at any time. Justin finished his coffee and stood, carrying his bag and leading Ethan out of the lounge to the boarding area.

More than a few people recognized him, but they kept their distance. He smiled and waved at them, presenting his boarding pass and walking down the Jetway. He got to his seat, buckled in, and closed his eyes. Sometimes he could ignore the activity and people talking about him if he simply shut them out.

"It's all right. People are going about their business, and everything is fine," Ethan told him.

Justin relaxed and smiled at the flight attendant when she asked if he wanted anything to drink. "I'm fine for now. Thank you." He smiled brightly at her, and she professionally went about her work. This was going to be a good flight. He'd had flight attendants who seemed flustered when he was around, and a few had been so excited they hadn't been able to talk to him.

The flight attendant gathered up the glasses and service items as the doors were closed and the captain made his initial announcement. Justin was about to power off his phone when it chimed softly.

Have a good flight. I miss you already.

I miss you too. Have fun. I will be back as soon as I can.

We will. I love you.

Justin's throat clenched when he saw those words. *I love you too*, he typed and pressed Send. Then he powered off his phone and put it in his pocket as the plane backed away from the gate.

THE FLIGHT was as comfortable as a cross-country flight could be. Justin rested and spent some time reading. He still owed Roy some answers and was determined to get them to him. Justin was never lucky enough to be able to sleep on planes, unlike Ethan, who zonked out for much of the trip. He did doze a little and woke Ethan as they were getting ready to descend into New York.

At the airport, they were met by a driver Marcheta's people had sent, and as soon as they had their luggage, they were whisked away to the Plaza and up to a suite overlooking the park. Justin would have loved to have had time to take a walk, but he decided on a short nap instead and let Ethan handle the schedule. He got twenty minutes of quiet before Ethan came in with a change of clothes.

"You need to change and clean up. The car will be here in fifteen minutes."

Ethan was his usual calm self, even as Justin's stomach was doing somersaults. He'd done hundreds of interviews and a number of live television appearances in his career, but this one seemed different, and he was at loose ends.

"Okay," he answered, trying to get his head into the game. He grabbed the clothes and went into the bathroom.

"I know you'd rather be someplace else, but you have to let that go for a few hours. Otherwise it will come through in the interview, and you need this to be positive," Ethan said through the door. "Just stick to what we talked about and enjoy yourself. You can do this."

"You can cut the cheerleader act. I'll be just fine," Justin called through the bathroom door as he finished shaving and washed his face. He dried his hands and put on his fresh clothes. He had decided on comfortable, casual clothes that would look good on camera. They had figured a suit would be overkill, but Ethan had one in a bag that would go with them in case that changed.

Justin finished dressing and left the bathroom, then sat on the edge of the luxurious bed to pull on his socks and shoes. He took a deep breath, wanting nothing more than to go home.

He let his second foot drop to the floor with a thud and felt his arms shaking. "I don't want to be here. George is back in LA, in my house. I finally have him out there with me, and I'm fucking here in blasted New York. I hate this shit, Ethan."

"I know, Justin. This is hard." Ethan handed him a coat. "I don't want to push, but we need to go, and you need to clear all that from your head."

"I'm doing my best, but I know I'm going to come off like some sort of idiot." He had never been this distracted or had his head so in a completely different place before an appearance, and it was scaring him. Justin wasn't sure how he was going to get it under control, though he knew he needed to quickly. He pushed himself off the bed and followed Ethan out of the suite, down in the elevators, and then out to a waiting limousine.

He managed to get his nerves under control while they rode, and by the time they arrived at the building where Marcheta's show was broadcast, he was feeling a little better.

The goddess of television herself greeted Justin with a huge smile and a warm hug when he entered. She was busy with preparations, so they talked very briefly, and then he went with Ethan to makeup. "The show will start in half an hour," one of Marcheta's assistants said. "When you're ready, I'll take you to the green room, where you can wait, and then I'll get you just before it's time for you to go on."

"Thank you," Justin told him while the makeup artist finished getting him ready for the cameras.

"You look great," she said when he was done.

Justin thanked her for her help and followed the assistant to the green room, where he paced like a caged tiger. This whole experience felt wrong, and he didn't know why, but he could feel it going very badly already. Ethan was nervous as well, and that only fed his own discomfort.

"Justin, you have to calm down or you're going to end up looking like Tom Cruise did when he jumped up on one of the chairs and acted like a monkey. You want to be able to set the record straight and stop the rumors and speculation in its tracks. To do that you need to come off well."

"I don't know why I'm so wound up."

"That's easy. It's because you don't want to talk about this. I suspect you've told George, but you never told anyone else. Now you have to tell the public something you thought you could keep private."

The thought left him cold. "But…."

"What is it?" Ethan said.

"What if I was the one who was wrong?" Justin asked.

"Where did that come from? Man. You were never wrong. You did what you had to in order to survive after your father rejected you and pulled the rug from under your feet. You had nothing, and you've made something of yourself."

"Yeah, but what if…?" It was so hard for him to give voice to fears that he knew weren't rational. Ethan was correct, and he was letting his doubts and worries eat at him.

"You did what you thought was right at the time," Ethan told him gently. "I know that in my heart, and so does George. If he doesn't blame you for what happened and is willing to move on, then you can take strength in that."

He was trying to, but it wasn't coming. "I don't know how I can go out there and talk about this in front of strangers." Everyone thought that actors could talk about anything and that they'd say anything to get attention. There had been plenty of examples of that in recent decades, but Justin was not like that.

"Then don't," Ethan said.

"Five minutes," Marcheta's assistant said from the doorway and then left.

"Then what? Just blow off the interview?" Justin was starting to wonder if Ethan was losing his mind. They'd come all this way, and now he was telling him to back out?

"No. I mean don't tell all those people out there what happened. Just tell the one person who knows and already understands." Ethan stood because their time before the interview was very short. "Just talk to George. When you're talking about what happened, just tell George. Don't worry about what anyone else thinks or who is watching. Just speak to George."

Marcheta's assistant breezed into the room, and Justin stood, leaving along with her to take his place in the wings while he waited for his introduction. All he kept thinking were three simple words: *speak to George.*

CHAPTER 10

GEORGE HAD watched all kinds of television shows. Many of his clients liked to watch television, and it was his policy that they should be as comfortable as possible, so they watched what the client wanted, and he often sat with them when he wasn't actively working. "Why am I so nervous?" George asked his mother as he sat on the sofa in the pool house. "I'm not the one giving the interview."

"Sweetheart," his mother said, patting his hand. "It's because part of you is in that interview. I keep wondering when you're going to see that Justin carries a part of your heart with him wherever he goes, just like you carry part of his."

"Isn't this show usually on during the day?" George asked, changing the subject as best he could. He didn't want to have a discussion with his mother about how he felt about Justin without talking to him about it first.

"Yes. I love her. Marcheta is from Lancaster, and she started on the station there. She does these evening specials when she has something she wants to say or someone extra important to interview." His mother would know all about it.

Applause pulled his attention to the television. "Put your hands together for the first lady of television, Marcheta Lewis!" the announcer cried, and the applause ratcheted up to a near frenzy. Marcheta took the stage at stride, accepting the accolades of her adoring fans, waiting for the applause to quiet.

"I'm so happy to be here this evening because I have the pleasure of talking with a good friend of mine. I first met him two years ago in Los Angeles, and he stole my heart. Our guest tonight is a dear man, and I am so looking forward to talking with him. Will you please welcome Justin Hawthorne?"

The applause ramped up to a fever pitch, and George's heart skipped a beat as Justin walked out on stage, smiling. Marcheta embraced him and then led him back to the chairs, motioning for him to take a seat.

"It's so good to have you here."

"It's great to be here. You are always an amazing hostess."

Justin smiled at the camera, but George saw the lines around his eyes that told him how nervous he was.

"And I've been trying to get you in my chair ever since we first met. But it seems you're a very busy man. I don't envy you your shooting schedule."

Justin chuckled. "And I don't envy you yours. I've heard you're one of the hardest-working people on television, and after what I saw tonight, I believe it." He flashed another smile.

Marcheta took the compliment like a lady, bowing her head slightly. "There are so many things I'd like to talk about, but I think there's something I have to ask to clear the air, as it were. There have been stories speculating about the circumstances of why you left home. You've said multiple times that you left Pennsylvania just before you turned nineteen and came to Hollywood."

"Yes, that's true," Justin agreed.

"We have some pictures of you," Marcheta said, and an image of Justin in his first role flashed on the screen. He was shirtless in a cameo on a television program, followed by a few other images, mostly chosen to highlight Justin's looks. "I can see why you made the Hollywood dream come true."

"Well, sometimes dreams have a start that isn't so pleasant." The camera returned to Justin, whose smile faded. "I left home at nineteen, a few days after I told my family I was gay."

Justin paused, and the audience was silent. George wondered if they were sympathetic or not.

"My father didn't understand or want a gay son, so I was forced to leave."

The camera panned in, and George wanted to rush to Justin so he could comfort him.

"Why did you come out to them?"

"I hadn't intended to, but I'd fallen in love for the first time. My best friend—his name is George—and I… our feelings developed beyond those of simple friendship, and I wasn't going to hide or deny him to my family. George deserved better than that. He always deserved the best care and love of anyone I've ever known, and I wasn't about to hide what I felt."

"What I think I'd like to understand is why you left if you had such strong feelings for George," Marcheta asked in a sympathetic tone.

"That's the hard question. You see, there were and still are other people in that small town who did not accept or like what I had told my parents. George's family is and has always been supportive, and I was on my way to George's after my own family turned their backs on me. I was stopped by one of the men in town and…."

Justin paused, and George held his breath.

"I have never talked about this except privately to a very good friend. But I was attacked and injured, by force." Justin took a deep breath. "Raped." He seemed to deflate a little as soon as he said the word. The audience made a collective gasp. "That's the first time I have ever been able to bring myself to say the word."

The camera panned out and showed Marcheta holding Justin's hands in hers. George leaped to his feet, wishing he could have been the one to comfort Justin.

She turned to the camera. "We're going to take a break, but we'll be right back." Her voice nearly broke, and George didn't move until Justin's image disappeared from the screen.

George reached for his phone and called the number Ethan had given him in case of emergencies. "Are you watching this?" he asked as soon as Ethan answered.

"Yes. I didn't know he was going to go into that. We hadn't talked about it. I thought he was going to talk about his father, the fight, leaving, and how they'd found some peace before his father passed away."

"He looked about ready to fall apart. You have to help him," George said. "Or so help me God, I'll beat the crap out of you when you get back out here."

"I will, George. I have to go."

George hung up and saw the logo for the show displayed on the TV screen. He sat back down next to his mother, nervous as a long-tailed cat in a room full of rocking chairs. The audience applauded, and the camera panned to Justin and Marcheta.

"We're back with Justin Hawthorne," she said. "Before the break you told us something very powerful and private. Why did you do that? You know you didn't have to."

"Because it was time to let it go and stop hiding and holding it inside."

Marcheta leaned a little closer to Justin. "There's more to this story, isn't there?"

"Yes. My attacker was the son of an important man in town, and he threatened George. He said he'd do to him what he'd done to me unless I got out of town. I know now he was afraid of what he'd done and getting me to leave was the only way he thought he'd be safe. But I couldn't let anything happen to George. I loved him… I still love him."

"So you left and came to Hollywood."

"Yes. I was helped by other friends on the way, and I used the hurt and pain as a well I could draw from when I needed it." Justin straightened up slightly, and his eyes became brighter.

"We've all seen your performances on-screen, and they are masterfully stunning." The audience punctuated Marcheta's statement with a round of applause that had to be deafening in real life. "So what happened with George? Is he still in Pennsylvania? Does he know how you feel?"

"My father and I made peace before he died, when I went back to see him. I was able to reconnect with George then, and I realized that even after years of separation, I still loved him. But I'd hurt him because of the way I'd left, and I think that's been hard for him to overcome."

"So is this a story with a happy ending?" Marcheta asked, and George leaned forward, wondering how Justin would answer. "We'll find out in just a few minutes." The show went to commercial, and George's phone rang.

"Yes, Ethan?"

"I need you to go into Justin's office and sit at his desk chair. I have activated the computer, and someone will be contacting you from the show. We'd like to put you on."

"Me? I…."

"Please, just go into the office."

"I'm in the pool house." He was already moving, with his mother right behind him. "I look like hell."

"I'm getting you a different shirt," his mother said as they entered the main house. George sat in the desk chair. The desktop computer was on, and he saw himself in a small box in the corner. His mother came in, and he pulled off the shirt he had on and shrugged on a fresh one.

"I'm ready."

"I'm going to watch the show." His mother left the room and closed the door.

"Hang up the phone and wait to be called back."

Ethan ended the call, and seconds later the screen came to life with an image from one of the television cameras. His phone rang, and he answered.

"George?"

"Yes," he said nervously.

"Excellent. We're going to patch you to the show in about three minutes or so. You're coming through well, and you look very good. Just relax. Please make sure that there are no televisions on nearby and that everything else in the room is muted. When we transfer you, all you'll hear is what's coming from the microphones on stage. So you'll hear Marcheta and Mr. Hawthorne. Speak directly to them. I'm going to ask you to hang up the phone so I can make sure we're getting sound from you, and we'll be good."

George nodded and ended the call, putting his phone in a drawer.

"Can you hear me?"

"Yes, I can hear you," George answered.

"Excellent. Now just answer the questions and realize there may be a slight delay. You won't be able to hear yourself on the screen to prevent feedback, but you are coming through. Can you see and hear them on stage?"

"Yes." George's nerves were getting the best of him.

"Just relax and don't be nervous. Marcheta is the best in the business, and she'll lead you through anything. Just follow her."

"Thanks."

"We're back," Marcheta said and turned to Justin. "You were going to tell us how this story ended, but we thought you might like to have a little help with that. So we have someone special who's going to join us."

The camera panned, and the curtain at the back of the set parted. George saw his own face there.

"I believe you know each other."

George smiled. "Hi, Marcheta, this is a bit of a surprise."

"Have you been watching the interview?"

"Yes. I was watching it with my mother at Justin's house in Los Angeles."

"That sounds promising as far as a happy ending."

"We came out to visit him during his break from filming, and he had to fly back to see you. I'm here anxiously awaiting his return."

"I see." She was all smiles. George liked her. "You were aware of what Justin said during the interview?"

"Yes. He told me some time ago. But he has one thing wrong. I do understand his reasons for leaving all those years ago. Justin is the bravest, kindest, most amazing man I have ever met." His voice was on the edge of breaking, and he'd be damned if he was going to let that happen on television. "We were young, and he was trying to protect me."

"What did you think when he came back into your life?" Marcheta asked.

"I was grateful and stunned at how much I still cared for him, and then by how much he loved me. Seven years is a long time to be apart, but that time didn't matter. But of course Justin had to return to his own life, and I wasn't able to join him." He was starting to feel a little more at ease.

"Have things changed?" Marcheta inquired.

"I like to think they have," Justin answered. "I know what's important now. Everything in life comes at some sort of cost. If you're a celebrity, then you forfeit some of your privacy. And sometimes there are other sacrifices to be made. But Georgie, you are worth more than anything else. I want you in my life, and I will promise to do my best to make you happy."

"I know you will. A few days ago you asked me a question, and I never gave you an answer. It was a very important question, and you deserve to know how I feel."

"Georgie, you don't have to give the answer right now."

"I will," George said. "The answer to your question is yes."

Justin leaped to his feet and punched the air in triumph. The whoop came through to him, and George grinned. "I love you, Justin," George said. Marcheta was all smiles, and George kept blinking to keep the tears at bay.

"I love you too, Georgie." There was obvious pandemonium because he could hear the echo of the audience through the microphones.

"We'll be back in a few minutes," Marcheta said and went quiet for a second. "That was amazing, George. Thank you so much for being with us."

"You're welcome."

"The next time I'm on the West Coast, I would love to meet you in person."

She smiled and had to know he could see it, and then the screen went blank. He pulled out his phone, and it rang a minute later.

"That was incredible."

"Thanks, Ethan."

"No. I mean it. That was so genuine and caring." He sounded as choked up as George was. "We need to finish up here, and then we'll go back to the hotel. I'm sure Justin will call you as soon as he can. In fact, I doubt anything could stop him from calling."

"Okay." George hung up and joined his mother in the other room. They watched the last portion of the interview where Justin talked a little about his upcoming movies. Then he and Marcheta did a brief wrap-up and the program ended.

"You were amazing, and you looked so handsome," George's mother said. "I thought you were going to cry for a few seconds there." She smirked at him. "You have to admit that I was right."

"You're going to say I told you so?"

"Okay, I won't. But that was one hell of a way to be told that you're loved."

"Oh, Mom." He hugged her gently. "I've always known I was loved. You and Dad made sure of that."

"I always tried, but the thing is, this is a different kind of love. I loved you as a parent. Justin loves you as a life partner, friend, and lover. I can't be there for the rest of your life, and you know that. Justin can and will be."

"Mom, are you trying to tell me something?" George asked fearfully.

"No…." She rolled her eyes. "I'm not going to depart this earth at any second, but I want you taken care of and happy. That's all a mother ever wants, and Justin will do that for you. Lord knows he makes you happy. Everyone can see that." She leaned closer. "That goofy grin you get whenever you look at him is enough to tell the world."

"Mom…." George's phone rang, interrupting the conversation, which was probably a good thing. "Justin."

"You didn't tell me you were going to be on the show," Justin began like a house on fire. "You should have told me."

"I didn't know. Ethan arranged it with someone from the show as it was happening. Suddenly I got a call and I was on television." The excitement was catching. "Did I do all right?"

"You were great, and I miss you so damn much. I have another interview in less than eight hours, and then I'm coming home. This schedule is killer, but I want to get back to you. We have a lot to talk about." Concern colored his voice.

"Actually, I think we covered what was really important on the show."

"Then you were serious?" Justin asked.

"Of course I was. Do you think I'm the kind of guy who would lie to you on national television?" George did his best to sound hurt, and Justin's laughter told him he'd made his point. "Get home as soon as you can. That's all I ask. I have to warn you—Mother is already talking about redecorating the pool house."

"I am not," she said from behind him.

Justin's laughter was forced. "I will." The fatigue was settling in to his voice.

"Go to sleep and call me when you get to the airport. I'll be waiting until you're back." He glanced at his mother. "I love you, Justin. We can discuss everything else if you want, but that's a simple fact."

"I love the simple facts," Justin said. "I'll see you tomorrow." He ended the call.

Shirley announced that she was going to bed. George saw her out and then locked up the house and curled up on the sofa, watching television until he felt tired enough to go to sleep.

IN THE morning, George watched Justin's morning talk show interview. It was much less formal, and they were kind and their questions tended to be more on the side of light entertainment. They talked about his upcoming movies and, of course, George. Justin was introduced to the joys of scrapbooking, and he went along with genuine happiness.

Adam reworked his schedule and showed up with his family when the show ended, and George and his mother rode with them to Disneyland. He and his mother had a ball with the mouse, and his mother rode the Matterhorn and Space Mountain, yelling right along with Adam's son and daughter, who thought Shirley was the greatest thing ever. George kept his phone on in case Justin called, but it remained quiet all day.

They stayed for the fireworks, and then Adam drove them all back. Adam's son, Joseph, fell asleep in his car seat while his daughter, Annabelle, leaned against Shirley's side. It was an incredible day of fun, and the cherry on top was the sight of Justin coming out of the house to meet them once they pulled into the drive.

"Did the interviews go well?" Adam asked Justin in a quiet voice after he lowered the window.

"Yes. I think you and I need to do a few shows once our film is set to release. Marcheta was particularly interested." Justin slid his arm around George's waist. "Thank you for everything."

Adam smiled. "It was a great day. I need to get the kids home. We'll do some shows together. I'd like that." Adam pulled out of the drive, and Justin guided George and his mother inside.

"I'm going to go right to bed," his mother said. "Don't you young people stay up too late." The smirk told George exactly what his mother meant. "I'm glad I'm in the pool house." She smiled and left through the back doors.

"Where's Ethan?"

"He's in the office, probably talking with Roy."

"Don't you need to talk to him too?"

Justin shook his head, eyes darkening, upper lip curling upward just a touch. "What I need is something much more important, so unless you want me to strip you naked right here, I think we better get to the bedroom... and fast." Feral cats had nothing on the energy Justin put out.

Primal, basic, animalistic, intense—all described Justin at that moment. George quivered and strode down the hall in order to keep ahead of Justin as he stalked after him. He managed to reach the sanctuary of the bedroom. Justin closed the door, took George into his arms, and pushed him back against it with a soft thud.

The door panels scratched into his back, but he didn't care at all. Justin pressed to him, his heat radiating through their clothes and skin to touch George's heart. This was his man, his mate, the person he'd spend the rest of his life with. George's pulse raced as Justin tugged frantically at his shirt. He probably lost a few buttons in Justin's haste, but once the shirt parted, Justin placed his hands flat on George's chest and sighed. "I needed to feel you."

"I'm right here, and I'm not going anywhere," George whispered.

Justin tugged George's shirt off and tossed it to the floor. He pressed hard, cupping George's cheeks in his hot hands. Energy and intensity coursed through Justin, who sent them straight to him. George tingled with it, and that sensation grew in intensity when Justin kissed him. Their lips dueled, and George pressed back, moving them away from the door. The scent of testosterone and sweat filled his nose, giving George a boost until Justin fell back on the bed.

"Jesus," Justin groaned.

George toed off his shoes. "You weren't the only fucking one who got wound up. I watched you on television talking about me, and I couldn't touch you." He opened his belt and pushed his pants down and off. "You damn near cried, and I wasn't there to comfort you." He kicked his jeans to the corner and stepped, naked, to the bed. "You went through hell, and I wasn't there." He climbed onto the bed. "Now, you have to the count of ten to get those clothes off, or I'll rip them from you." George shook with desire that increased as Justin moved at near light speed. Clothes flew right and left, and as soon as the last stitch hit the floor, George pounced.

Justin caught him in a tight embrace, their bodies pressing, sharing heat, passion building. Justin stroked his back and over George's ass, cupping him tightly as they ground their hips together. There was no way George could stop.

"I missed you so much."

"Me too."

Justin held him tighter, rolling them on the bed. George locked his legs around Justin's waist. This was no time for slow and leisurely. He needed Justin badly. Somehow George got the drawer by the side of the bed open without it falling to the floor. He grabbed a condom and shoved it into Justin's hand. He needed the connection so badly his hand shook.

Justin moved away, and then he was back. His fingers sank into him, disappeared, and then Justin pressed forward. George arched his back, groaning as Justin slid home. George was complete, heart and body joined.

"I need you, Justin. I know that now. Being without you is like being starved for air. My soul needs you."

Justin held still inside him, his hips pressing to George's butt. "I need you too. I can make movies without you, but I know now I can't live, really live, without you. I was missing part of myself all those years, and it wasn't until I saw you again that I knew what I'd lost." Justin slowly rocked back and forth, bringing George along with him. "I need you."

"I want you." George pressed to Justin, grabbing his ass, pulling him closer.

"I can't live without you." Justin withdrew and plunged deep, stealing George's breath.

"You're the other half of me." George's voice rasped as Justin's cock scraped over the spot inside him, sending him to the stratosphere.

"I love you."

Justin's control slipped away, and George knew he was in for the ride of his life. In the bedroom, out of it, they were the same. Their love had stood the test of time, distance, and age. They were different people, and through it all their love survived. It might have dimmed at times, but it had never died, and George knew it never would. He tightened his hold, pulling Justin into a sloppy kiss that made him happy to be truly alive.

EPILOGUE

GEORGE OPENED the door and stepped into the house—their home—with Justin right behind him. "That was something else. I see why it took so much out of you," George said as he pulled off his black bow tie and loosened the collar of his tuxedo shirt. Movie premieres, with all the glamour and flashbulbs, were a little overwhelming, but Justin had stayed with him the entire time.

"There's already Oscar buzz," Ethan said as he walked past them. George barely noticed. "Okay, I can talk about all that later." He continued on through to the living room, and George lost himself in Justin's eyes. "I got a message from the moving company, and they found your missing box. It's going to be delivered tomorrow."

"Thanks, Ethan. That only took them three months." The cross-country move had been hectic, but everything had been packed, shipped, and moved into the house in LA. What surprised George was how little he had that he actually decided to move. He and his mother had sold most of the larger things to lighten the load.

"I know." Ethan grabbed his laptop and left the room. "I'm going to work for a while and then go to bed. I'll see you all in the morning." Ethan waved and disappeared into his bedroom.

"Say hello to Tom," George called.

"I will," Ethan agreed with a happy lilt in his voice.

It had taken George some time to get used to having Ethan living with them. He liked Ethan well enough, and he'd taken good care of Justin for a lot of years, but there had been tension between them at the start. Mainly because George wasn't sure of his role in Justin's life. Ethan managed a lot of Justin's time and business, and to George it had felt intrusive. But he and Ethan had come to an understanding, and things had worked out well. It hadn't hurt that Ethan had met someone a few months ago and was developing a life of his own away from George and Justin.

"I'm glad he's happy," Justin said as he watched Ethan leave.

"Me too."

"I owe him a lot."

"I know. Ethan is a wonderful person, and I'm glad he and I worked things out. He took care of you when I wasn't around, and I'll always be grateful to him for that."

Justin took his hand and led George down toward their bedroom. "I thought we'd take a swim before bed." With Shirley and Ethan living with them, they'd pretty much given up skinny-dipping, but they both loved the quiet time in the water.

"That would be nice," George agreed, leaning in to soak up some of Justin's heat.

He was still so keyed up, and George knew it would be hours before Justin was able to sleep. Justin closed the bedroom door, and George took off his jacket.

"Stop," Justin said, turning around. He was still fully dressed and looked incredibly handsome in his tux. "I've been trying to ask you something all night, and I could never find the right time. I was going to do this before we left, and then time got away from us."

"What is it?" George asked, concerned that something was wrong.

"Georgie," Justin began and then knelt on the carpet. "I want you to be part of my life forever. I know I asked you to move here, but you took up permanent residence in my heart a long time ago."

George blinked as Justin reached into his coat pocket and pulled out a small box.

"Justin."

"I want to ask you to marry me." He opened the box to display a sparkling man's diamond ring. "Will you wear this to tell everyone that you're mine and you'll always be mine?"

"But I don't have one for you," George croaked around the lump in his throat as Justin took his hand and slid the ring on his finger.

"We'll get one if you like," Justin said. "Or we can go down and pick up matching wedding bands."

Justin kissed the back of his hand and then slowly stood back up. George wrapped his arms around Justin's neck, shimmying closer to share a kiss.

"Of course I'll marry you," George said, barely believing he was answering that question. He'd never expected a proposal.

"Don't cry," Justin whispered, but he ended up wiping his own eyes. Then he tugged George close for another kiss that curled his toes. "I love you, Georgie."

Swimming was completely forgotten, and words were no longer needed as they showed each other just how long their love would last… forever.

ANDREW GREY grew up in western Michigan with a father who loved to tell stories and a mother who loved to read them. Since then he has lived all over the country and traveled throughout the world. He has a master's degree from the University of Wisconsin-Milwaukee and now works full-time on his writing. Andrew's hobbies include collecting antiques, gardening, and leaving his dirty dishes anywhere but in the sink (particularly when writing). He considers himself blessed with an accepting family, fantastic friends, and the world's most supportive and loving husband. Andrew currently lives in beautiful historic Carlisle, Pennsylvania.

E-mail: andrewgrey@comcast.net
Website: www.andrewgreybooks.com

CHASING
THE
Dream

ANDREW
GREY

Born with a silver spoon in his mouth, Brian Paulson has lived a life of luxury and ease. If he's been left lonely because of his family's pursuit of wealth and their own happiness, he figures it's a small price to pay for what he sees as most important: money.

Cade McAllister has never had it easy. He works two jobs to support himself, his mother, and his special-needs brother. They don't have much, but to Cade, love and taking care of the people who are important to him mean more than material possessions. When Cade is mugged in the park, he can't afford to lose what little he has, and he's grateful for Brian's intervention.

Cade is given a chance to return the favor when Brian's grandfather passes away and Brian's assets are frozen. Cade offers Brian a place to stay and helps him find work, and the two men grow closer as they learn the good and the bad of the very different worlds they come from. Just as Brian is starting to see there's more to life than what money can buy, a clause in his grandfather's will could send their relationship up in smoke.

www.dreamspinnerpress.com

FIRE AND Water

ANDREW GREY

Carlisle Cops: Book One

Officer Red Markham knows about the ugly side of life after a car accident left him scarred and his parents dead. His job policing the streets of Carlisle, PA, only adds to the ugliness, and lately, drug overdoses have been on the rise. One afternoon, Red is dispatched to the local Y for a drowning accident involving a child. Arriving on site, he finds the boy rescued by lifeguard Terry Baumgartner. Of course, Red isn't surprised when gorgeous Terry won't give him and his ugly mug the time of day.

Overhearing one of the officer's comments about him being shallow opens Terry's eyes. Maybe he isn't as kindhearted as he always thought. His friend Julie suggests he help those less fortunate by delivering food to the elderly. On his route he meets outspoken Margie, a woman who says what's on her mind. Turns out, she's Officer Red's aunt.

Red and Terry's worlds collide as Red tries to track the source of the drugs and protect Terry from an ex-boyfriend who won't take no for an answer. Together they might discover a chance for more than they expected—if they can see beyond what's on the surface.

www.dreamspinnerpress.com

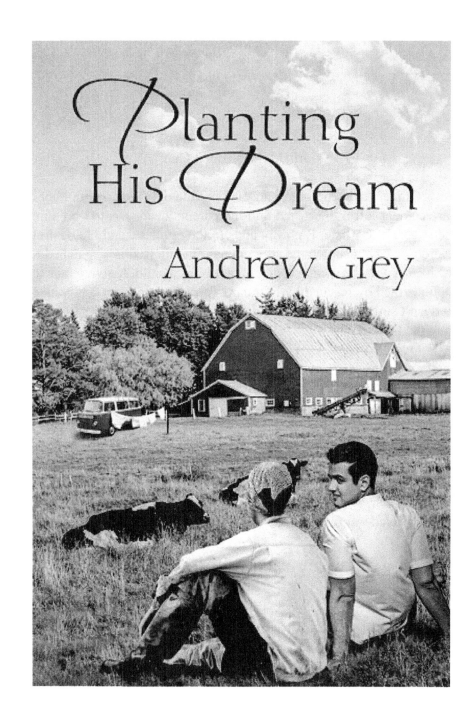

Planting
His Dream

Andrew Grey

Foster dreams of getting away, but after his father's death, he has to take over the family dairy farm. It soon becomes clear his father hasn't been doing the best job of running it, so not only does Foster need to take over the day-to-day operations, he also needs to find new ways of bringing in revenue.

Javi has no time to dream. He and his family are migrant workers, and daily survival is a struggle, so they travel to anywhere they can get work. When they arrive in their old van, Foster arranges for Javi to help him on the farm.

To Javi's surprise, Foster listens to his ideas and actually puts them into action. Over days that turn into weeks, they grow to like and then care for each other, but they come from two very different worlds, and they both have responsibilities to their families that neither can walk away from. Is it possible for them to discover a dream they can share? Perhaps they can plant their own and nurture it together to see it grow, if their different backgrounds don't separate them forever.

www.dreamspinnerpress.com

REKINDLED FLAME

ANDREW GREY

Firefighter Morgan has worked hard to build a home for himself after a nomadic childhood. When Morgan is called to a fire, he finds the family out front, but their tenant still inside. He rescues Richard Smalley, who turns out to be an old friend he hasn't seen in years and the one person he regretted leaving behind.

Richard has had a hard life. He served in the military, where he lost the use of his legs, and has been struggling to make his way since coming home. Now that he no longer has a place to live, Morgan takes him in, but when someone attempts to set fire to Morgan's house, they both become suspicious and wonder what's going on.

Years ago Morgan was gutted when he moved away, leaving Richard behind, so he's happy to pick things up where they left off. But now that Richard seems to be the target of an arsonist, he may not be the safest person to be around.

www.dreamspinnerpress.com

ANDREW GREY

TURNING
the PAGE

Malcolm Webber is still grieving the loss of his partner of twenty years to cancer. He's buried his mind and feelings in his legal work and isn't looking for another relationship. He isn't expecting to feel such a strong attraction when he meets Hans Erickson—especially since the man is quite a bit younger than him.

Hans is an adventure writer with an exciting lifestyle to match. When he needs a tax attorney to straighten out an error with the IRS, he ends up on the other side of the handsome Malcolm's desk. The heat between them is undeniable, but business has to come first. When it's concluded, Hans leaps on the chance to make his move.

Malcolm isn't sure he's ready for the next chapter in his life. Hans is so young and active that Malcolm worries he won't be able to hold his interest for long. Just when he's convinced himself to take the risk and turn the page, problems at the law office threaten to end their love story before it can really begin.

www.dreamspinnerpress.com